The Hamlet in the Hills

Keith Harris

Published by Pending Press Ltd.

The Hamlet in the Hills

All non-historical characters in this fantasy novel
are fictional,
any resemblance of these characters to living persons
is purely accidental.

This book is published by Pending Press Ltd.

ISBN 978-1-903466-07-0

Til Fruen Vår

All shall be well,
And all shall be well,
And all manner of thing shall be well

– Julian of Norwich

Prologue
An Oasis in the North

June 2149 in the broad shallow valley where I lived in the middle part of my childhood, a few miles from what had once been Trondheim. Nearly a thousand years earlier this Norwegian city had been a major centre of medieval pilgrimage. Today even its cathedral stands in ruins; no choirs sing there, only wind and rain, and the harsh shrieking of carrion gulls disturb its broken nave.

Though the sun had set and the sky was without cloud no stars were visible. In these northern climes twilight lingers in the deep of Summer night. I sat on a stump of wood gazing at her seven-sided green and rose-red crystal which had been carefully embedded in granite to mark the place where her ashes had been mixed with earth. Soon flowering plants would hide both crystal and stone, and only a few of us would remember Lihana.

Some years had passed since I had last seen her, since I had last breathed deeply in the resin fragrance of this Northern Oasis. Our colonies, our Oases as we call them, are dotted around the globe. Our communications are a secret only known to the seers and initiates.

The wars destroyed technology, destroyed humanity's cultural and industrial heritage, and brought an end to electrical networks of virtual pastime and control. Pollution became out legacy.

Plant life can grow even over chemical waste. Nuclear waste is worse. And worst of all are the manipulated organisms as they propagate themselves. How many were made? Tens of thousands, most were viral, bacterial or fungal organisms against which nature's plant and animal life had limited defence, though numerous crops, flowering plants and higher animals also underwent genetic modification.

In the later stages of the wars dinosaur DNA was isolated, spliced and laboratory specimens brought forth. And they were getting ever closer to producing self-propagating nano and pico mechanisms.

Yet in the final analysis not even the Falarchs, the False Architects, were to blame. We ourselves, billions of men and women, let them go ahead with their plans. Our hearts and minds were attuned to screens while 'the experts of science', as they styled themselves, told us their experiments and their productions would bring purpose, peace and plenty.

Now we live with the consequences.

Though their central command was broken in the middle of the last century, the monsters of their manipulations still reproduce, still feed upon and breed with nature's own species.

At the beginning of the twenty-first century mass vaccination programs of girls in pre-childbearing age began the attack which made it ever harder for women to have children. How many human beings are alive today? It is not known for certain, definitely less than a billion but perhaps only two or three hundred million live upon the earth.

Ever we defend ourselves against the Hordes, ever our hearts bleed for the men, women and children in the Blighted Lands who are neither of the Oases nor the Hordes.

Today as I sat near her ash-stone I thought about my earlier life and resolved to relive it. He once told me it would be good if I learned how to inherit my own life, even as human beings at the end of days needs must inherit the earth herself and the deeds of all nations.

All we have undergone is still alive in our etheric bodies. To live in recollection is to live in the etheric forces of our own being.

To uncover memories from the period between three and seven years of age is no easy task. The experiences of those times respire in the depths of sleeping consciousness and should not be disturbed without good cause. Delving into these memories brings about a certain division, because what once happened, is experienced by both the little child you were and the individual you are.

I try to rediscover the day when my conscious memories first awoke and live through it again.

1. The Hamlet

No one told me where I came from. No one ever asked.

He brought me to the hamlet while I was still a toddler. We called him Grey One. Faded grey his garments, grey his bushy hair and short-cropped beard, his brown eyes sea-grey flecked. He was a traveller, one of the few in those days who braved the woodways and the ridgeways.

Our little village, the hamlet, lay in the foothills, above the forests, below the white frosts and the snow. Rough-hewn mountain stone overlaid with compact earth on which plants grew, grass upon the roofs, our dwellings nestled into nature. From the eves of the forest almost half a mile away only a keen eye would have noticed these were homes and human made. The hamlet was surrounded by birch, rowan, taller thorn bushes and evergreen shrubs.

There were two teenagers but I was the only young child in the village. Its fence marked the limit of my life. It was strictly forbidden for children to pass through unaccompanied. I would watch as the workmen left to cull forest trees but none of them ever winked or beckoned me to follow. Within the boundary though I was free to roam around between the twenty or more buildings, the gardens, the sheep pens, the barns, the chicken runs as I wished. I knew every stone and plant within the perimeter.

In the hamlet we waited. Always we seemed to be waiting … waiting for the Winter's end, the next batch of food, for the storms to stop, for news from the Rangemen … and I waited for the Grey One's visits.

As a young child alone in the house senses his mother's absence and as his longing for her homecoming deepens to an unspoken fear that she might never return – so I waited for him to visit us. My heart only belonged to the hamlet when the Grey was there. When he left, part of me fell away gently into dreaming or forgetfulness.

2. A Walk on the Wildside

There came a moment in my early life which marked the closure of unconscious childhood. The Grey One ever exhorted me to recall the events of that day – the first day of conscious memory. And I have often tried to picture what did happen. It was the day I was given my first play-practice.

Monika woke me, sitting on the bed and gently shaking my shoulder, her greying hair as ever in a tight bun.

The Grey says you may begin to toss balls, an enigmatic gleam dwelt in her eyes as she stroked my hair. How old was Monika? Late thirties, forties perhaps even fifty. Her age as her expression was hard to guess. She was not tall but stood straight and dignified. Her play-practice was to dance.

Throwing! Can I start learning how to throw?

Not throwing, most certainly not! You are far too young. You can learn to toss balls and later learn to catch them. She sat me at the table and ceremoniously placed a ball of tightly packed uncombed wool into my left hand. It fitted perfectly into my palm. She got me to transfer it to my right hand then to put it on the table. Three balls placed into a neat triangle. *They are yours. If you lose them you will have to make new ones yourself.* She explained how I was to loop them underarm into a basket, pitch them against a wall and throw a ball in the air and try to catch it.

I sat looking at the balls imagining there were ten or more and that I was effortlessly juggling with them. Her voice interrupted my daydream, *Well go on, try them.*

I jumped up, underarmed a ball at a basket in the corner and missed, pitched the second hard up the wall and got the rebound back in my face, tossed the third up in the air and made a grab at it far too late.

She shook her head, *You have a lot to learn, Kell, I am not so good with children maybe the Grey can give you a few tips when he comes back.*

I was only allowed to practise for half an hour and then had to put the balls carefully away into a draw.

Known as the Watcher's Chair, a rock jutted out from the cliff side behind and to the left of our village. Once in a while a guard or even a Rangeman might be seen there. Ascending to the stony seat was difficult and in frosty weather dangerous. When the Grey One visited he might sit there motionless from mid morning to late afternoon. Some said his gaze searched over forest and lake into far distances, others that he was listening, listening to the world's wilfulness and woe.

At the end of my session of play-practice I had tossed a ball into the air and caught it twice in succession. I so wanted to tell him about it. Outside in the chill of early Autumn I discerned his figure motionless upon the Watcher's Chair. It was hard to get absorbed in play because I kept looking to see if he were still there. Hours might have passed when I finally saw he was gone. I knew he would come back to the village and I thought I knew the path he would take. I ran to where it opened into the hamlet. My body throbbed with expectation, I looked around but saw no one … and then I resolved to go out and meet the Grey One.

In front of me were two tall rose bushes, one bearing many red blooms, the other three or four white roses. They stood on either side of the path and formed an intertwining arch above it. My heart pounded as I took tentative steps toward it, Never before had I left the village by myself. Monika had again and again reminded me not to leave.

Now as the afternoon began to fade I, a three year old child, walked by myself toward a path leading out of the community.

I felt sure that once I had passed under the living arch of roses I would be able to see him and run to him. I jogged joyfully under the arch and along the pathway which curved imperceptibly to the left.

Not many paces further along I detected the change; the undergrowth thinner, the light dimmer, the homely airy fragrance of the hamlet was replaced by the odour of decay, mould and fungal rot. I heard noises, scratching, scraping, scampering, clicking insect sounds. Something slithered across the path behind me. I ran on blindly. A twig scratched my face, another tore at my sleeve. I turned back and could no longer see the arch of roses – in this instant my earlier life closed behind me.

A huge wasp droned toward me. I ran on, though the path was becoming indistinguishable from the surrounding thicket. Then came the howl, the blood-chilling cry of a creature of the night. My body stopped. Blind fear held me in shock. Part of me wanted to cast myself into the rotting undergrowth and disappear or even die, part of me yearned to cry out with human voice.

The wasp circled menacingly around me. A sharp pain jabbed my arm, a large black mosquito had stuck its proboscis through my jacket.

Gr, Grey, the sounds coming from my lips were barely audible croaks yet they steadied me, my child's voice called clearly and strongly, *Grey One*.

I listened to the echoes.

The scraping and slithering settled. I sensed a silent inwardness within me. For one long moment I waited. Then I heard the singing, the rhythm and melody of the setting sun, the language was unknown to me. Within the space of heartbeats the song became clear and vibrant. The creatures of the wild, insects, rats, snakes, all flew, scampered or slithered away from where I stood, just as animals might flee a forest fire.

The Grey One appeared.

And it was lighter.

The mosquito, which had been greedily sucking my blood, flew up from my arm. All at once, as a bird pierced through the breast by an arrow, it fell from flight into his outstretched hand. He closely observed its crumpled form for a few seconds before tossing it with disgust into the undergrowth and turning to me. With an expression of utmost yet tender seriousness he looked deeply into me. I was afraid I had done something very wrong. His surprisingly soft hand brushed away my tears. He ruffled my hair, his eyes sparkling with merriment.

Now you see how dangerous throwing can be! You have only been practising for half an hour and already you've cast yourself out of the community.

A shiver shook me, my legs trembled, I reached up to him. He picked me up. I was clinging tightly round his neck. Warmth filled my chest and spread through me.

They have missed you, he whispered, *We must return*. When the rosy arch came into view he stopped and set me upon my feet. *Now you can walk through by yourself.*

I let go of his hand and took a few tentative steps toward the threshold becoming aware again of chill and the smell of decay but as I walked through the archway the fragrance of roses and the homely scent of village earth drifted to my nostrils.

I heard a shout and saw Monika swiftly striding toward me. She seized my arms, her face distraught with anxiety, *Where, where have you been?*

Monika, be still, the Grey's voice was quiet. We turned

to see him beside us. She let go of my arms and rose to her full height looking straight into his face as he spoke, *He has come to himself in the wilds.*

A wave of understanding seemed to pass between them. Tears came to both their eyes.

Without further word he took my right hand, she my left and we walked toward the hall. It was Thursday, the evening of the High Feast.

3. Kaspar

Next morning a lump the size of half a walnut bulged on my arm where the black gnat had bitten me. The Grey One examined it, shaking his head and frowning. His voice was gruff but a smile softened his lips, *A child cannot expect to go walking alone on the wild side and come back unmarked.*

A potion was made for me which tasted of bitter herbs. He added a few drops of a clear liquid from a tiny flask taken from a pocket in his cloak.

His visit was longer than usual and he spent time telling me many things.

You hear about someone you have never met and involuntarily a picture of them is conjured forth. When you later actually meet that person, you are aware of the radical difference between their physical appearance and the impression created earlier in your mind.

Yet if I chanced to meet for the first time a person, the Grey One had previously described to me, the resemblance between how they looked and my earlier imaginative picture would be astonishing. How closely did the person match the way I'd imagined them to be – not only as regards outer appearance but inner animation.

When he told me about something, it was as if I walked with him into the events themselves. Everything was detailed with a stability we normally only associate with the outer world but very much more alive.

On the day before he left as we walked holding hands from the High Meal, he said he had a surprise for me. Men had been hard at work building something onto Monika's dwelling. As we approached he gestured toward it, *It is finished, would you like to look?*

We opened the door with a creak. Inside a shaft of pale moonlight shone through a barred window. The smell of drying mortar and oiled wood met us as we crossed the threshold. For a three year old the room was big. He lit a candle on a little table. There was a bed and a sturdy chair low enough for a child to sit upon. The room felt new and, with his presence, warm.

Do you like it?

I nodded.

We shall sleep here tonight.

I cannot really recall where I used to sleep before this time, I think it was in the home of Monika.

He sat down upon a thick woollen rug, I snuggled up beside him.

If you heed me this will be your home from now on, little one. He held me closely and began to tell me about Kaspar; it was as though I left the building we were sitting in.

We seemed to be in a busy township from a time before cars or locomotives. Traders were shouting loudly in a tongue I recognised as German. In the hamlet a Scandinavian language or English were generally spoken but when I was alone with Monika, she invariably spoke German to me.

Horse-drawn carts crossed our way. He whispered to me that we were in the early nineteenth century. We walked into quieter streets and entered a large house. A maid ran down the stairs and passed us. I felt very shy and drew into him. He smiled at me, *We are in a story which really happened. The people here cannot see us.* He took me along a darker passageway and pointed down at the wall, *Look closely.*

I discerned a low door which blended into the

woodwork covering the wall and knew that behind the door was a dark space.

Little more than a hole. You could stand but a growing boy would be forced to sit were he imprisoned in there. Let us, as many before, bring a little light into this tragic history.

As I gazed, the space behind the wall seemed to grow lighter. I don't know how but I could see into the hole. A little boy was sitting there in what to physical sight would have been pitch darkness. In his hands was a wooden horse which he lovingly caressed.

The Grey One pulled my arm, *Let us move on.* We climbed stairs. He lifted me up to look out of a window. It was dusk, the blue sky deepening, stars beginning to appear. Lights could be glimpsed through the windows of the houses. *Yes, little one, people in this town went about their businesses giving no heed to the tragedy taking place in their midsts. A child imprisoned from before your age for two thirds of his life in a dark cramped hole in the wall.* He paused and looked out of the window again, I turned my head in the same direction. The sky was now black, the stars shining in a cold crystal-clear night. *Come let us look again at Kaspar, the boy who from the time his memories awoke never saw the stars.*

We descended the stairs. As we moved toward the hole I had a sensation similar to walking back from outside into the hamlet through the arching roses, as though carrion dark crowded around his solitary space wilfully striving to engulf him but that he, to use the language of grown-ups, sat bathed in angelic radiance.

Once more I was able to see through the hidden door and discern the boy who appeared to have grown into a teenager. He was shivering but holding onto his wooden horse as though to warm it. I pulled at the Grey One's

garments and wanted to plead with him to releas[e]
As though in answer to my unspoken question [h]
his head solemnly.

From further down the passageway a door opened letting in light. A figure appeared, swarthy and unshaven with shaggy hair. Instinctively I wanted to draw away and hide. The Grey held tightly onto my hand and I remembered we were in a history and the man was not able to see us. He carried a lamp, a blanket and a bag. He stopped beside the door to the hole, set the lantern down, took a bottle from the bag and poured liquid into a cup.

It is only water, the Grey One whispered.

The man took a crust of bread and set it beside the cup then he blew out the lamp and stood for a few moments as though waiting for his eyes to adjust to the darkness. He stooped down and unlocked the hidden door. I could see, I don't know how, the boy inside. As the door began to open a look of joy transfigured his face and inarticulate sounds broke from his lips, he tried to push forward and reach up but the man put his hand on Kaspar's head as though to stop him from emerging. He tossed the rough blanket into the hole, put the cup inside and shoved the crust of bread in with his foot. The man's surly features seemed to soften involuntarily as his hand ruffled Kaspar's hair. Then he grit his jaw, shoved the boy's head down to the floor and closed the door. For some moments he stood there, his eyes beginning to fill with tears, suddenly he shook his fist at something or someone far away, grabbed the lamp and stumbled back along the passage in the dark, opened a door and closed it. We looked, I don't know how, through this door and saw him go into a kitchen. He poured himself a tankard of beer from a wooden barrel and swallowed a great mouthful. Another man was wrestling on the floor with a giggling scullery maid.

The Grey One spoke and my sight reverted to the darkness around us, *Thus does he swill his guts with ale and pour his conscience into his belly.*

Behind the secret door Kaspar was offering his horse water and then the crust of bread. He gave it a cuddle then sipped from the cup and took a bite of bread himself.

As I looked up at the Grey One the history disappeared and we were sitting again in my new room in the hamlet. I threw myself into his chest and felt myself crying uncontrollably.

After my sobs had subsided he brushed back my dark hair and began to sing soothingly. I saw again the man, who had fed Kaspar, angrily shaking his fist. *Who did he shake his fist at?*

The planner's, the architects of that crime, he broke off the sentence and looked at me significantly, *Yes, they are as active today as then.*

I wanted to ask more but he stood up and blew out the candle, *Let us take a sip of water and a bite of bread in the dark, in memory of Kaspar Hauser.*

Only after we had taken a sup and gone outside to walk upon the moist earth, smelled the greenery and gazed up at the stars – those stars the imprisoned boy never saw after his memory awoke – was he prepared to speak to me again. We were back inside my room seated upon the rug. *If you hearken to me, you will live here, live here alone – in memory of Kaspar Hauser – if you would grow to be a Kasparian knight.*

A profound longing arose within me, I threw my head onto his knee, *Let me live in a little hole like him.*

He chuckled heartily, *No, little one, you cannot bear such a burden. And why should you? Kaspar has borne that not just for himself but for us all.*

I glanced up at him, *What's a knight?*

He sighed, *You know nothing of King Arthur and his Knights of the Round Table, Lancelot, Parsifal, Galahad ... but, em, you do know about princes and princesses, don't you?*

What's a prince?

Has Monika not been telling you fairytales?

I shook my head. He let out a low whistle. I heard a dog bark. *We must have a chat with her,* he said.

A few moments later there was a tap on the door. He opened. Monika stood there with a shawl around her shoulders, behind her I caught sight of Djorki.

Djorki was one of the hamlet's dogs. I had always been a little afraid of him. His colouring was reminiscent to that of a Welsh collie, his bark deep and resonant, his height was that of a St Bernard though he was much sleeker, and he was proud. Imagine if an adult encountered a dog whose size could dwarf a shire horse and you'll realise why as a three year old I didn't go too near him. The Grey One loved him though.

As Monika came in he gave the dog a hug and got his face licked. He closed the door. Djorki remained outside. She sat down on the rug. He spoke to her in English, *You are invited, dear Monika, by the little one to partake of bread and water,* and he added casting me a smile, *He wants to hear about knights.*

The nights are cold and dark but if he is afraid, I can pull out the connecting panel and comfort him. She stood up and held a candle to illuminate the small oak panel separating our dwellings. *If you are frightened, call to me and I will remove this and sing to you, Kell.*

He chuckled, *Yes Monika, very good but he would like to hear about King Arthur's knights – and he needs to be told fairytales, he needs to hear about princes and princesses.*

He woke me before dawn. I was still half asleep as he lit a candle and sat me on his lap. *I will soon be leaving. Do you remember the boy they hid the stars from?*

I closed my eyes and pictured Kaspar sitting in the secret closet with his wooden horse. *Yes, Grey One.*

Do you remember that I spoke to you of living here alone?

To become a Kasparian knight, I answered eagerly.

He smiled broadly, *Yes!*

Who are Kasparians?

They are not like knights of old. Unknown to the world they wander.

Are they Rangemen?

He gazed into the distance, *Many a Rangeman is walking a path toward knighthood.*

But who is a Kasparian knight?

He looked at me long and thoughtfully before answering, *One at least you know.*

I understood he was speaking about himself.

A deep powerful bark broke the pre-dawn stillness.

Djorki, he muttered, *What is afoot, my friend?*

He stood up and lifted me back into bed. A moment later a sharp rap sounded on the door. He opened, a Rangeman standing in the shadows gave him a whispered message. He nodded, picked up his cloak and turned to me, *Sleep now.*

When I woke I knew instantly he had left the hamlet and that I should wait long before seeing him again. I was on the point of breaking into tears when there came a knock on the door.

C, come in.

Monika unlatched the door. She stared at me with her unreadable Slavic features. Her voice was stern, *From now on part of your required play-practice will be to listen to fairytales.*

4. Time Trickles By

For the next couple of years I only met the Grey One occasionally. His visits were brief. Sometimes he would arrive in the night, wake me in the morning and be gone before the sun had set. Yet he seemed satisfied with my growing up. If he stayed longer he would sleep on the floor in my little dwelling which like the rest of the village was built of dry stone with mortar on the inside and pressed earth on the outside. The roof sloped down from the wall connecting my room with Monika's. There was no heating as such but the large Finnish brick-built stove in her home was in this wall and in it a wood fire always burnt so even in the depths of Winter's snow my room was never cold. The only entrance was a sturdy oak door opening on the side away from the forest and toward the rising rock of the foothills. A little shuttered window was opposite the door; from the door to the window measured about five grown-up paces, from the connecting wall to the lower wall opposite about four paces. It was furnished with two chairs, a table, a cupboard, a bed and on the wall by the window hung a rough-hewn wooden cross.

Half my early childhood was spent in this room.

The Grey Ones' place in my heart was as both mother and father. Monika was my custodian. My relationship to her must have been like that of a child sent away from a war zone to stay with a strict maiden aunt.

Play-practice with the woollen balls continued to be severely limited. But every morning and evening Monika told me fairytales. Whenever I asked about learning to juggle, throw or tumble, she would purse her lips and say, *Play is the best play-practice for you.*

Once just after a morning fairytale as she was on her way

to the hall to practise dance, I chased after pestering her to be given more daring play-practice. She stopped in her tracks, looked down at me and asked, *Do you recall the giant in yesterday's story?*

Yes.

What colour was his shirt?

Green with big dirty brown buttons.

How do you know that he didn't have a blue shirt with ivory buttons?

Er, I looked up at her with my mouth open.

You see, Kell, you are creating pictures, pictures you have never seen before. She glanced toward the forest and spoke as though she were addressing a different audience, *Before the catastrophes they strove to rip inner picturing away from children*. Her voice became earnest, *But this is like tearing a babe from the breast. The child's forming of inner pictures is food, without this their health and their spirit will not develop aright. They*, she almost spat the words as she said them, *The False Architects, had all manner of outer pictures made, screens with moving scenes, anything to take children away from creating their own inner pictures*.

She turned back to me, *You are conjuring, you are conjuring forth inner pictures, this is a magical process, it is play-practice of real quality. So be patient, Kell. Although I am a fine one, you might think, to be preaching patience!*

Her expression changed almost as though she were about to smile as she asked, *Shall I teach you to dance?*

No, dancing's for girls! I want to fight. Can you make me a sword? I slashed out with an imaginary knife.

She made a tutting sound, *Dancing is more dangerous than you deem!* And with that she turned away and departed.

When I spoke to the Grey One about new kinds of play-practice, he asked me why I lived alone in my little room. I answered proudly, *In memory of Kaspar Hauser.*

Very good, he replied, *Remembering Kaspar is play-practice of the highest significance.*

So whenever I had nothing to do, I thought about Kaspar in his hole. I even played with him. I imagined myself creeping along that passageway, opening the secret door and showing him the little woolly lamb I slept with. He wasn't able to speak so we gestured to make ourselves understood. I told him about the stars and how one day he would leave this little closet and see them himself. His eyes glistened faintly in the darkness as I whispered about the heavens revolving above us.

Once after a rainy Autumn day spent mostly by myself I asked Monika if I would ever become a knight.

No one knights themselves, Kell. When the time is ripe we will be knighted – whether the world ever knows or not.

I had the Grey One, I had Monika, and in a way I had Kaspar as well, but the other people in the hamlet never seemed to want to talk to me or have time for me in any way. I had lots of questions – and asking questions, well, children asking questions was not something done in the village. If I asked a villager a question, they would invariably stare at me for a moment or two, shake their heads as though the question was too dumb to deserve a comment and walk away.

It was only much later that I realised it was because Monika was in charge of me and they were afraid of her.

5. Creatures from the Wild

Early Spring around the time of my fifth birthday, the snows were beginning to melt but only a few flowers had sprung up.

One night a man, I had never seen before, came into my shelter and pulled me roughly out of bed. *Get dressed now!*

I put on my trousers and tied my shoes, *Where's Monika?*

No questions, brat, or you will feel the back of my hand.

He grabbed my arm and dragged me up. I kicked him as hard as I could in the shins. He must have struck me because I remembered nothing else before coming around in the hall. A fire was blazing. Two of the guards were tied up, one of them was lying unconscious. The villagers were cowering around the wall away from the fire. Four newcomers were sat at the table, a huge fellow with a patch over one eye and sleeves rolled up to his elbows was devouring a leg of lamb.

The door burst open, Monika appeared. She glanced around, saw me then strode toward the men at the table.

Well, well, what have we here, a woman who might be lucky enough to warm my bed tonight, the big fellow got up from his seat as he spoke and stepped toward her. Monika stood rock steady, she seemed to be straining to contain her anger. Still holding the leg of lamb in his left hand he reached out with the other to take her by the hair. She made a sudden barely perceptible movement with her elbows, there was a sound as of a branch cracking. The man cried out, one of the bones in his right forearm protruded up under his skin.

Another man drew a firearm but she had already picked

up a pepper pot and with a swift gliding motion it shot from her hand and hit him between the eyes. His smirk died as he slumped over the table. The two others were backing away toward the fire, the older one drawing a huge hunting knife. Monika took a step forward and made a flinging movement with her hands. Flames leapt out of the fire engulfing them both. The hair of the younger man was alight, the clothes of the older one smouldering and starting to burn. She picked up a jug of water and tipped it over the head of the younger one to douse his hair. To the older man she shouted, *Out, out roll in the dirt.*

Two of the guards stormed in, Djorki at their heels. The dog leapt toward the one with the broken arm.

Djorki, her voice sounded calm, the hound stayed itself and came obediently to her side.

The teenager was on his knees, wet hair falling over his brows, he was pointing at her, *She's a witch, a witch.*

She ignored him and turned to the villagers, *Disarm them*. Then she came to me. My lip was swollen and bloodied. *You have seen enough this night, Kell. Take Djorki and try to get some sleep.*

The dog came to me and licked my face.

I was glad to have him lying by my bed as I tried to forget my headache and fall asleep.

Next morning Monika called the whole village together. The miscreants were sat on chairs. Three guards stood behind them. Djorki stood proudly beside her as she spoke, *Three of the guards and I were away when they came last night*. She gestured to the intruders, *They have assured me that they have not come as part of a greater troop of pillagers and therefore may be allowed to sleep outside the village. Two of them are still in need of care.*

The one, who had taken the pepper pot between the

eyes, sat moaning with his head in his hands. The big fellow with the patch was ashen grey and slumped in his chair. The teenager was blabbering manically to himself. But the eyes of the older man were hard and calculating as he spoke, *Let us keep our weapons, we will do you no harm but if wolves attack we will be eaten if we cannot shoot.*

She stared at him stonefaced, *You have disgracefully broken the peace of the hamlet. Weaponless you will go forth. Wolves are noble creatures, fire will guard you from them. If a pack of wargs – spliced wolves – are on your trail, these puny weapons will avail you little. As long as you remain on the perimeter of the hamlet you will receive our protection. But unless you stand in great need of medical care you will be turned forth between dusk and dawn. You have after all disgracefully broken the sanctuary of a homestead.*

I did not see Monika again until after it was dark. She came to my room after the communal meal was over. *There are things afoot, Kell, the Rangemen have warned us of strange movements of animals. I have to be on guard so I will not be able to sing to you if you awake afraid in the night.*

I nodded bravely but felt more like crying. She put her arm round me and pulled me into her.

Monika, can Djorki sleep here tonight?

She frowned as though considering, *Well perhaps the danger is not so pressing and, who knows, it might be good for you to learn to befriend animals*.

Shortly after she left, I heard a bark outside my door. I opened it just enough to peer out. Djorki pushed the door back with his great paws and barged in, making me fall on my bottom.

He lay beside my bed with his head between his front paws, looking at me with eyes that might have been smirking.

In the dead of night I awoke with my heart pounding. Djorki was barking furiously. I opened the door for him and put on my clothes. When I came forth into the chill darkness the village was in uproar. Dogs were barking, sheep bleating and men with burning torches were running about. I heard Djorki's deep and unmistakable bark and stumbled toward it. Three of the intruders had come back into the village, they were shivering and seemed to be in terror. Behind them I saw Monika at one of the entrances to the hamlet. Djorki was beside her as was the elder of the two teenagers of our village. He was holding a torch. I moved closer to them.

A howl whose like I had never heard, a howl of unabated malice came from the darkness beyond the hamlet. It was answered by Djorki's bark which carried with a lion's power.

Come, said Monika as she stepped forth into black night.

Djorki was on her left, the teenager with the torch on her right. I found myself involuntarily following. She was moving her arms gracefully and swaying slightly as she stepped a dance form. As her movement came to a halt, the flame from the torch flared up brilliantly the height of a man above us in the air.

All around were wargs, fifty or more. Wolves, wolves with eyes of death. They backed away from the flame. She seemed to be wholly concentrated on the fire, she lifted her hands and it rose up ten, twenty feet above her. Our teenager was sweating with fear, glancing back and forth between the wargs and Monika, all at once he dropped the torch and lurched back toward the hamlet. The magical flame died, an ordinary torch lay burning on the ground.

A great warg launched itself from the left toward her head. Djorki took it by the throat. She made a cutting movement with her left arm, the warg's skull split, but the other wargs closed in.

Three guards with torches in their hands ran out and made a triangle about her. She steadied herself and repeated with utmost rapidity the earlier movements. As her motion was brought to a stop, the three torch flames rose up together, merged and leapt a further thirty feet into the air. I fell back from the searing heat. Her hand gestures seemed to be moulding the flame above her. It became an intense ball of fire. Her hands were lifted up almost as if they were holding the fire with an invisible force. Suddenly she flung her arms down and outwards, the ball of flame burst asunder into bolts of fire which cascaded into the wargs. Some were caught and burnt alive on the spot, others broke away in wild frenzy with their fur aflame.

Monika was left standing, a woman within a triangle of three guards each holding an ordinary torch. Stars were visible above us. The wolves were gone.

I heard a commotion behind us and turned to see a warg, which must have entered the hamlet by another entrance, catch one of the smaller dogs in its jaws. Djorki was upon it tearing at its throat. All at once the younger of our two teenagers rushed at it and thrust a wooden spike into its belly – and it was all over.

Monika had taken my hand and was marching me back. We passed the elder of the teenagers, the one who had dropped the torch, he cringed away from her. She passed him by without a word.

She had me in bed before she spoke, *Well Kell, once*

more you go where you should not be! But she held my hand tightly in both of hers and didn't seem cross.

I looked down at her hands, hands which had moulded magical fire. *You were wonderful.*

I was an oaf who nearly lost a battle that would have left us undefended.

But he dropped the torch and ran away.

Bah! The Grey can make fire out of nothing. I have not been attendant to my duties. She dropped her head. I squeezed her hands. *You see, Kell, fire exercises bring anger upon me. I have fought for years to control it*. She rose up, *Sleep now, I must see to the clean up*.

She was framed by the door as I asked her, *Aren't you a bit tired after making all that flame?*

Silly! she seemed, amazingly enough, to be on the point of smiling, *The hidden worlds are not bound by the Second Law of Thermodynamics, I do not make the energy out of myself. It is not tiredness the magician needs to fight against, it is elation – and inflation – and that craving, we are all prone to, to use magical means to further personal ends ... one day*, she added enigmatically, *I will tell you about the Empty Mountain*. Her hand grasped the door handle as she spoke, *Sleep now, Kell!*

Was that a magical command?

For the first time I remember, she actually smiled. *Silly*, she muttered closing the door and leaving me in the dark.

I pulled the woollen quilt tightly around me – and tried to recall the boy who spent two thirds of his life in a hole.

6. Rangemen

When she came in to tell me a fairytale next morning she looked as though she had been crying.

What's the matter?

I am a foolish old woman. I thought the four intruders were hale enough and if any one of them was in danger, it was he who took the pepper pot between the eyes. The youngest, only a teenager, I think, his mind was unhinged, he wandered away into the night. He will never be found, I fear. I should have understood his plight. How could I have missed it?

I did my best not to try to imagine him walking in the dark, talking to himself … as the wargs came.

What are wargs, where do they come from?

Nature does not bring forth such creatures, they were man-made.

But why would anyone want to make such beasts?

Why indeed! Foolish and dogmatic Darwinians, biologists who thought they could cut up life's nuclei and patch them back together – spice, patch and engender – and all without any consequence. But the planners, the False Architects, Falarchs we call them, they had their far-reaching purposes, their well-defined ends. She shook her head sadly, *It was us though, human beings on every continent who just let them do it. Petty scientists, the media said were experts and who even called themselves experts, came forward saying their experiments would bring the end of hunger and disease. People listened to their crafty spin and forgot the wisdom of the heart – and thus the spliced zone came into being, wargs and worse.*

She lapsed into silence. I wanted to ask questions but couldn't understand enough even to do that.

Kell, you need a holiday. So do I perhaps.

Am I that tough to teach?

She rubbed my ears till they were warm.

Stop it, stop it, I yelled.

Come let us walk in the sunshine.

As we walked around the hamlet gazing at flowers which had sprung up from the soil, I asked her, *Monika?*

What?

Will you teach me how to dance?

She stopped dead, stooped down so her face was level with mine and tapped me three times on the chest with her forefinger, *You just want to sprout fire and crack bones – you will have to find much better reasons than that, young man, if I am ever to teach you to dance*.

After the business with the intruders and the wolves, the attitude of the people in the hamlet toward me changed. Before they were reserved, after they avoided me like the plague, almost as if I had been a changeling planted on them by bad fairies. The two teenagers, who I think may have been apprentices training to be guards, left suddenly. And they were the only ones who would easily exchange words with me. A whole day might go by without me speaking to anyone but Monika, and with her only a few sentences. She seemed worried and reverted to her maiden aunt roll. I found myself thinking more and more about Kaspar in his prison.

Djorki was usually away on errands with the guards. But when he was in the village I often went to him. Such a great proud animal, he let me touch him but I didn't feel I could chase him around or take him for walks. I started to speak to him. I could tell him about what I hoped I would be when I grew up, I asked him about clouds and butterflies, anything and everything. One day after I had been telling the dog lots and lots of things, I turned to see her standing behind me.

Monika, er ... have you been listening.

She didn't answer.

Have you been there a long time?

Long enough! Come, Kell, it's like I said, you need a holiday.

Two days later the Grey One came to visit. He said he would take me for a stroll.

Except for the few steps taken behind Monika as she took on the wargs, I had not been outside the perimeter of the village since the day I came to myself in the wilds. He told me there were five gateways to the hamlet. One of them was marked by the arching roses and it was through this that I first left the community; he said that might be significant.

We went through this same gateway on my first outing to the Rangemen. He stopped before it. There were buds but no rose had yet to burst into flower. He asked me to walk through by myself, I hesitated.

Remember Kaspar, he whispered.

My limbs loosened, I walked determinedly under the arch. As before as soon as I stepped over the threshold the atmosphere changed. A wave of colder, rotting damp rolled over me. I went on a few paces and turned. He was not to be seen. Something like panic rose up in me. I heard a noise above me to my right, a spider, whose legs would have stretched across my five-year-old palm, dropped an arm's length down its web and began grappling with a wasp the size of a hornet.

His hand was on my shoulder, his face bore a look of loathing, he shook his head as he spoke, *Survival of the Fittest*.

Over the years, through incidents and through stories,

he made me aware of the world outside the hamlet – and of what we meet when we pass the archway. Once when I was much older, he described this as a harsh and abrupt encounter with the spliced zone.

A few hundred paces away from the village I began to be aware of another change. The undergrowth thinned, decaying smells gave way to fresher breezes. The sense of threat lifted. I was walking outside in a nature which may have resembled that of a century or more ago, in those times before genetically manipulated organisms began breeding rapaciously in the wilds.

What is happening, Grey One, why does it change so suddenly after the roses and why is the menace not here?

On the border of the hamlet two warrior natures are locked in combat. About us is a frightened nature, a nature the two warriors war over.

As we journeyed further up the foothills, we occasionally caught sight of birds which winged away to hide in bushes. Sometimes he would pick me up and carry me. After a couple of hours we sat on a little ridge and looked down. Far away now was the impenetrable forest. He pointed out the hamlet. From this vista it seemed almost as if the woods were striving to engulf the village, as though it were a dark wave of sea water surging to surround and wash away a sand castle on the beach.

He took a flask of water and a little roll of bread from a deep pocket and shared them between us. I had been both thirsty and hungry but after a couple of sips and a few bites, my thirst was stilled and my hunger satisfied. I sat on his grey cloak and nestled up to him as he began to sing. I felt heavy, warm and tired. Birds settled near us, tiny mice and even a couple of rabbits crept toward us as though eager to hear his song. A sleepy sensation grew on me.

When I woke it was growing dark. I heard voices and tried to get up but found myself wrapped in furs.

Your little bundle is alive, Michaelleon. I glanced up at the smiling face of a young Rangeman. It was my first sight of Raynor.

The Grey strode over and lifted me up. We were in a glade surrounded by silver birches. A camp fire glowed in the centre. Wisps of whitish smoke rose up toward the deep blue sky above us. Two Rangemen near the fire laughed heartily. Laughter, laughter! Hardly anyone in the hamlet ever laughed. Only when I was alone with the Grey One did we laugh together. I had spent more time with Monika than any other human being and could barely recall her giving more than a wry smile.

Time to eat, friends, boomed the deep voice of a jolly-faced Rangeman who must have been the cook. About a dozen Rangemen gathered around the fire, we joined the circle as well. I was half expecting lengthy prayers and silences as took place at the High Meal but the cook just took a little stew in a wooden spoon and spoke, *Let us give thanks to the stars and the spheres, to the shining sun, to the wind and the rain and to the goodness in the earth since–*

I couldn't make out the last word. He tossed the spoonful of soup into the air and let it fall to the ground. Then with a hearty chuckle he began to ladle broth into bowls for the Rangemen. Thin light bowls made of a substance I did not know. I caught the smell of herbs and vegetables, grains floated in the thick soup.

Memories of that evening drift as in a dream. Above all I remember the merriment. They joked even with the Grey One. In the hamlet people deferred to him and treated him to displays of respect but except for Monika and perhaps one or two of the guards I do not know if they loved him.

With the Rangemen he wholeheartedly joined in their fun. At one point he cast off his mantle and put a scarf round his head – suddenly his posture altered, he was the actor become an old woman with screechy voice and lifted forefinger who did a comic duet with Raynor playing her recreant son.

Later one of the Rangemen took out a small harp or lyre and began to chant. Do I remember or just imagine that I saw then in my mind's eye the beautiful daughter of Melian dancing under the stars in the magical woodlands of Doriath.

At one point the Grey One stiffened, turned toward the trees and touched Raynor's arm. From the place where he was looking, a figure appeared clad in similar raiment to the Rangemen. Raynor leapt to his feet whispering, *Ahwenda*.

The song stopped. The figure moved silently toward the firelight, cast the hood back and looked around the circle, *Greetings Grey One, greetings fellow Rangemen*. Her voice revealed her to be a woman. Her hair was fair. She gave Raynor a momentary shining smile. Soon after this she left the circle with the Grey and two older Rangemen. They spoke long and earnestly together.

Raynor drew closer to me, *Well, how do you like us, we who wander in the wild woods?*

Never had I imagined a world where people roved, joked and made music. Hitherto my life had been contained in the hamlet. I wanted to answer him but tears flooded over me. I covered my face with my hands and cried.

And I remembered how Kaspar cried on that night when he first saw the loveliness of the starlit heavens.

After a minute he spoke again, *Are we so frightful?* His face bore a wide smile.

No, I glanced across to the group around the Grey One. Ahwenda was looking inquisitively at us. *Er, er, who is Ahwenda?*

Ahwenda, he paused, *She is our messenger, fleeter than any of us. She can run with the deer. Maybe the Grey can roam more swiftly than she, but none of us here.*

The Grey One, I said wonderingly. I had never imagined him running.

In the light before dawn Raynor woke me, *You will be leaving shortly. I have offered to bear you back to the village but the Grey says he will take you home himself. You are his friend and thus you are my friend. We Rangemen possess very little but ... here*. He handed me a stone similar to an iron-age arrow head. It fitted nicely into my palm. *It is a calling stone – part of a Rangeman's trade. I am not allowed to give you a finished stone but keep this in memory of your visit to us*.

Ahwenda came up, *What secrets are you two sharing?*

I just gave him a stone, not a finished one of course.

She touched my hair and looked at me keenly, her eyes were blue-green, *I will give him a kiss*.

Soon after I was in the Grey One's arms and we were on our way back to my village. I saw that we had been in a valley. None of the surrounding countryside was recognisable. I guess we were as far away from the hamlet as it would take a hiker to walk in a day.

Dawn pink lightened the Eastern horizon as we came to the head of the valley. He held me snugly, our pace rapid, his movement smooth even as the eurythmy of Monika. After a while we chanced upon deer. The herd raced away along the path at our approach, the undergrowth was thick on either side, he quickly closed in on them before staying his pace until the woodland thinned and they ran off the path.

The rosy hues faded into the blue skies of morning as we reached the ridge where we had lunched yesterday. He put me down so we could observe once more the hamlet and the forest behind it stretching into the far distance.

Grey One, that story about Lu, Luth–

Luthien and Beren.

Was it true?

It comes from a story, its author might have said it is to be found in the foliage of the Tree of Tales. Is it true – when is it not true, little one?

But did it happen?

Did it happen, you ask, mm, their encounter and their love lives in the legend so you could say it happened in the story. Yet, he paused, *In the high vaults of the world's memories this tale is not to be found near Kaspar's actual deed. The Rangemen are moved by the tale because they live in the twilight between the loveliness of the Oases and darkness of the Hordes. The Silmarilian and the tale of the Ring provide the kind of significance for them which Greek myths held for the Romantic poets*.

Even he spoke to me sometimes as if I were grown up.

He smiled down at me, *But you are not versed in history. Come.*

And before I could ask one of the many questions stirring inside me, he had picked me up and we were quickly descending toward the hamlet.

A short while later we stopped. From a change in the air I thought we must be nearing the rotten undergrowth around the village. We walked hand in hand until the rosy arch came into sight.

Here you walk by yourself. Always leave and enter upright and upon your own feet. Tell Monika, I am come and departed again.

Just before the threshold of the roses I turned back and waved to him then I marched through into the fragrance of the homestead.

Something big bounded passed me. I lost balance, tumbled and rolled over in the moist earth. Glancing back I saw Djorki disappear down the path I had entered by. I heard his joyful barking.

As I tried to clamber to my feet I became aware of someone standing over me.

Monika, I, em, I–

She looked at me with narrowed eyes.

The Grey One said, he came – and went.

She continued to look at me without a word.

I saw Rangemen and, and, and–

Doubtless they thought your clothes were too clean.

Before I could answer, she had taken my hand and was marching me away. I knew where to … and that it was no use arguing. She opened the door of the hut which housed the washing stream and guided me in.

7. The Hunya-Hunya-Hunyas

Late Spring. The men began building a large new dwelling in the hamlet. When I asked Monika about it, she told me it was a guest house and added that people would be coming from East, West, North and South, and that some would break their journeys with a short stay in the village.

People came. Men and women speaking one of the Scandinavian languages, German, English, Russian or another Slavic tongue. Monika told me my play-practice that Summer was to listen to the newcomers. She encouraged me to approach the travellers and speak to them. As the only child in the village I found myself a centre of attention. Most of the travellers only spent a night or two in the hamlet before they left. If they stayed longer, one of the villages would invariably corner them and whisper something so that their attitude toward me changed overnight. They would shun me. After a few such hurtful incidents, I decided I wouldn't let them turn their backs on me any more and went back to playing by myself and talking to Djorki.

Monika told me a Celtic fairy tale about a changeling who grew up not being able to find his place among people he knew. A being stranded between two worlds. This story affected me deeply. I started having nightmares and stopped even talking to the dog. One day I went up to Monika resolving to ask her the question whose answer I feared.

Can I ask you something?

Of course. She seemed in a good mood after dancing and was still wearing a silk dress.

I hesitated, too afraid of what she might answer and turned away, *No, nothing.* I wandered away in the direction of the rosy archway.

Kell?

I didn't stop.

Kell!

I started to run. A moment later she had her hands on me.

Let me go, I want to leave.

What is the matter with you young man? She wasn't going to let me loose.

Monika?

Yes.

Monika.

Yes, just tell me, Kell, what on earth is the matter with you?

Monika, am I, am I a changeling?

What?!

I thought I knew what her answer would be. I dropped to the ground and covered my ears with my hands.

She lifted me up. That was definitely not a Monika-thing, she never picked me up. She carried me further toward the archway of roses. I was sure she would be turning me out, taking me to where the fairies could carry me off but I didn't care. If I was a changeling I would never find a home in the hamlet or among human beings.

A few steps from the threshold we stopped. One or two of the buds were breaking into colour.

Kell listen, you are not a changeling. We are related you and I, and I am no fairy.

That she definitely was not. But what did she mean about us being related? Perhaps she really was my maiden aunt?

What made you think all this nonsense about being a changeling?

I told her about how the villagers would speak to the travellers and how after that they would just ignore me.

The villagers, she shook her head sadly, *But spreading malicious gossip – that will definitely have to stop!*

I think she must have called a meeting or something and told them in no uncertain terms that the whispering had to cease, because after this none of the travellers shunned me.

At Midsummer the hunya-hunya-hunya couple arrived. They were young, joked and had fun. They laughed, they laughed! Laughter free and fair sounded in the hamlet. The villagers shunned them. But the young couple didn't shun me, I was treated as a prince and a playfellow. They loved talking to me and teaching me the hunya-hunya-hunya dialect.

Monika called it the hunya-hunya-hunya, because when they said 'a hundred she-dogs', it sounded like: 'hunya hunya hunya'. They were from Trondheim, or from that region where the city once stood, and spoke the Tronder dialect of Norwegian. They remained for five or six weeks and by the end of their stay I was fluent in their dialect.

The villagers resented them. Whether because Sten and Kristina were able to have fun and laugh or whether it was because they spent time with me, I do not know. One day some of the villagers came up to Monika and demanded that the couple work. Travellers always worked if they were able-bodied and stayed for more than a day. About eight or nine villagers stood in a half circle around her. Dungbjorn – the biggest man in the hamlet, sort of grumpy, shaggy, not fond of washing and himself only a recent arrival – seemed to be their spokesman. He must have weighed three times as much as Monika. His voice was raised, *They have to work, they eats our food and sleeps in our beds, they work must!*

She was her stone-faced self. After giving him chance

to speak, she answered curtly not in his broken Norwegian but in English, *They are working; they are helping to bring up the child. And bringing up children is a most essential work.*

Dungbjorn let out a stifled, Agh-sound and seemed to reach out toward her. Luckily – lucky for him, I think, for I had seen what she did to the last man who tried to lay a hand on her – Djorki gave a lion bark. And Dungbjorn was forced to take a grip on himself.

The villagers drifted away as she stared at them. She was left standing alone. Djorki padded up and shoved his muzzle under her arm.

8. Miss and Moppar

Kristina was stooping to pick a flower as she asked me what I would like to be when I grew up. I immediately thought about Kaspar and mumbled something about a knight. She was sniffing the flower, from the expression in her eyes she might have been far away and not really listening, she turned to me smiling, *I want to be a mother!* She laughed, *How foolish that would have sounded a century ago. People had children whether they wanted them or not. Sten and I just want to have a child.*

Only one?

Silly! We would have ten if we could, then added a little sadly, *But no one can be certain of having children today.* She picked another flower, brightening up as she twirled it in her fingers, *Up to now we've only managed to have cats. Come on let's see if we can find Miss and Moppar.*

They had brought two large Norwegian forest cats, Miss and Moppar, with them. These cats were much bigger than the ones in the hamlet and they had thick fur to withstand the wind and snow. Miss, the she-cat, was white. Moppar had a touch of forn in his fur. The cats were friendly but you couldn't just fondle and fool around with them. They were proud and independent animals. And they seemed just as much at home outside as inside the hamlet.

Sometimes I would watch them as they left by one of the hamlet's entrances. Once I even decided to follow them. But I felt Monika's hand on my shoulder, she must have been watching me as closely as I watched the cats.

Going somewhere?

Er.

Just remember, Kell, curiosity killed the cat.

Will they be killed out there?

Those two! I very much doubt it. But it would be quite a

different matter with a little child like you.

They nearly did get slain though, not outside but inside the hamlet. Dungbjorn's mutt, which smelled almost as bad as its master, was at the head of a pack of dogs which cornered the two cats near the washing hut. Moppar leapt up and clawed his way onto the roof but as Miss jumped, the mutt sprang at her snapping at her fur, she twisted in mid-air and lashed her claw across his nose drawing blood. But as she fell the other dogs attacked. It all went so quickly, I thought she would be ripped apart. She was on her back spitting and clawing.

Then everything seemed to stop. There was a loud bark and the dogs sort of froze. Djorki was among them. He tossed one of the dogs into the air and growled as he approached Dung's mutt. Have you ever seen a dog pee itself? All the other dogs fled, Dungbjorn's rolled over and sprayed itself. When Djorki didn't attack, it gave a yelp and ran off with its tail between its legs. That night it probably did stink as much as its master.

I came up and patted Djorki, and gave him a hug when he tried to lick my face. Moppar jumped down from the roof and came to us with his tail in the air. He pushed around my legs and began purring. Then he brushed against one of Djorki's legs still purring. The dog looked down at him and pulled his leg away. Moppar was purring very loudly as he pushed up against another of the dog's legs. I don't think a cat had ever pushed itself against Djorki and purred before. He looked down and sniffed the cat. Miss miaowed, ran over to us and started pushing herself up against my leg.

The next time I saw the cats, they were sleeping beside the sleeping Djorki. After this I don't think any of the dogs ever dared to attack the cats again, not since they had Djorki's scent on them.

9. Summer Draws to a Close

Travellers came and didn't ignore me. Djorki, Miss and Moppar were my playfellows. Even Monika appeared less weighed down. And with Kristina and Sten almost always with me, I must have experienced a little of how children live when they grow up with parents.

When you are young, somehow you think life will go on as it is. Summer seems everlasting. But changes come whether you will or nil. For better or worse, life is always in motion.

The hours of daylight began to lessen, the night sky was dark. One afternoon in late Summer a dozen or more people arrived from the Baltic region speaking a Slavic language. They were travelling West. Next day I saw little of Sten and Kristina. Djorki was away so I spent most of my time with the cats as they jumped around after butterflies between the flower beds.

At the end of the evening meal Kristina gave me a hug and didn't let go, *Kell, it's been so lovely being here, playing with you, sharing in your childhood*. She had tears in her eyes. *But tomorrow we have to say farewell. We are leaving with the travellers going West. We want to find a place on the sea shore where we can bring up a child,* she bit her lip and added, *Children*.

Sten put his hand on my shoulder, *The stars have returned, let us walk under them. And let us say, as they do in my favourite book, 'May a star shine on our parting'*.

I felt too numb even to cry.

Kristina came to my room in the early morning. *Kell, I want to tell you about a dream I had last night. An angel came to me bearing a babe. I so wanted to take the child but as I reached out the angel shook its head. And I knew somehow that I had first to give something up. When I woke, I knew I would leave Miss and Moppar for you, if you want them.*

As I waved goodbye I was shivering. The cold of night resided in the morning air. Winter was fast approaching. Winter in the hamlet with snow and darkness, with the villagers, without travellers, without Kristina and Sten, and only Djorki, the cats, a maiden aunt … and Kaspar for company.

10. Friends Come Visiting

That Autumn the Grey One came to visit three or four times. And though when conversing with Monika he often seemed grave, with me he was full of playful fun. He took me further into the life of Kaspar Hauser. We watched together as the fifteen year old Kaspar wandered into Nuremberg on Whit Monday in 1828, hardly able to walk, not able to speak. We saw how some wonderful people took charge of him and helped him. We witnessed how he could repeat a long poem after only hearing it once. And how he came to be called 'the Child of Europe' … that Europe which might have been.

Thinking back on those times makes me aware of how isolated Monika was. Maybe she needed his visits almost as much as me. I sometimes wondered why she lived in this village when she could have wandered freely with the Rangemen.

As the snows began to fall and the days grew shorter the Grey One came to visit us again. I was watching the flames in the stove when he told us he was needed in the South and that we would see him no more before the Spring. Next morning the Rangemen came with a great batch of food to last us through the Winter. And he was to depart with them. I no longer cried when those I loved left, I only felt a numbness spreading though me.

The Rangemen were assembled on the snow outside the hamlet. I saw Raynor who called out to me and waved. The Grey gave Monika a hug then he knelt beside me and asked, *Do you have friends?*

I *have Miss and Moppar, and Djorki and Monika*, I paused before adding, *And Kaspar.*

Good. You are growing in the way of chivalry. But I am

going to leave you with another friend.

He kissed my forehead and went to sit on top of a dog sleigh. The Rangemen were on skis, they moved swiftly slanting across the sloping ground, the sleigh following behind. Djorki ran after the Grey. Soon they were out of sight. A single figure from their number remained standing, motionless, gazing after the Rangemen long after they were gone. Monika stood beside me, we waited as well.

The hooded figure turned and came toward us, moving with surprising swiftness for one not on skis. Something was familiar about the man – or woman, for as the hood was thrown back I realised it was Ahwenda. Her eyes were shining though perhaps shining with tears. She embraced Monika and put her hand on my head. I heard Djorki bark as he bounded back toward us.

We were drinking herb tea in Monika's home, mine with a spoonful of malt syrup, when Ahwenda told me she would be staying for the Winter, *I can't always be a message bearer for Rangemen. I am here to learn new tricks. I am to be an apprentice.*

What are you going to learn?

Dancing.

When I saw her in a perfectly fitting silk dress, I thought I had never seen anything so lovely. She was much taller than Monika but just as slim. She was willowy and with a standing jump could do a somersault over Djorki's back. And though there was something in the atmosphere of the hamlet not conductive to laughing, when she was alone with me we had lots of fun, even fits of giggling. I had hoped she might sleep in my room, as the Grey did when he visited, but she stayed with Monika.

More than once I saw Monika smile unreservedly when she was together with Ahwenda. Something cut into my heart when I witnessed this, a feeling which at first I wasn't quite able to put into words. Then I realised it must be because Monika loved Ahwenda more than me. Once I had grasped this, I was able to let it go. I guess I never really thought of Monika loving me, not as the Grey One did, or even as Djorki or the cats did; she was ever with me but part of her always felt a little withdrawn. Anyway it didn't matter if she loved Ahwenda, because I loved Ahwenda too. Truth to tell, I was in love with her as far as it is possible for a five year old to fall in love.

Once as she stood gazing at the lingering light of sunset I told her she must be the most beautiful woman in the world.

She gave me a strange half-smile and said, *I've seen someone much more beautiful than me.*

Who can that be?

Don't you know?

I shook my head.

Li, er I mean, Monika.

Monika? I could have used lots of fine words to describe Monika but beautiful would not have been one of them.

Funny how when you're young, time not only seems to go slowly, you also tend to think people have always looked the way they do now.

How old are you, Ahwenda?

Nineteen, nearly twenty.

When you were as young as me, did Monika still have her beauty?

She took my hand and we walked a few steps crunching through the snow. She was looking at me out of the corner of her eye. *Kell, has the Grey ever taken you into, well, has he ever told you a story which came alive?*

I stopped dead and nodded, *I've been with him to see Kaspar.*

She seemed deeply touched by what I'd said, *Yes, I have been to see Kapsar with him too but I was much older than you when he took me to share moments of Kaspar Hauser's imprisonment.*

Did he, did he ask you, er, did he speak to you about, about becoming–, I didn't know how to continue.

About becoming a Kasparian knight? Yes, he did. It seems women can be knights as well as men today.

I would be honoured to fight beside you, Ahwenda, I said in a very grown-up sort of voice.

She responded by lifting me up under the arms and throwing me high in the air and as she caught me, she twizzed around, *There's much more to being a knight than fighting.*

I was holding tightly round her neck as she walked on, a serious note sounding in her voice, *What do you know about Monika, Kell?*

All I know is that she is here.

Nothing else?

I shook my head.

Then it is not my place to speak about her. I will only say this, the Grey One took me back into her earlier life. I saw he when she was young, beautiful and so full of life. She could play the violin, the piano, speak half a dozen languages, she was an internationally recognised mathematician, she – I must say no more, Kell. Let the Grey or Monika tell you more if they wish.

After setting me back on my feet, she asked what I knew about my own life.

I shook my head, *I don't know nothin'. I think I've always been here ... unless the fairies brought me.*

She laughed, *Oh, Kell, you are a funny one! They'll tell you more when they think the time is right. I will tell you this though, we are orphans you and I.* She went silent looking off into the distance. The stars were beginning to gleam. Her breathing left a mist in the frosty air. She turned to me, *I knew my mother. I was your age, five years old, when she died.*

As I lay in bed, I wondered which is worse, never to have known your mother or to have lost her when you were only five. Somehow I found myself thinking about Kaspar's mother ... and about whether she ever held her newborn babe.

In the night I dreamt of Kaspar's birth, of his mother – of how they took Kaspar away before she ever held him, and how they came and gave her someone else's baby. Another babe whose breath they later stole away. I woke from this dream in the blackness of night. Everything had seemed so real. I thought I would ask the Grey One about whether what I'd dreamt had really happened. I was crying but decided not to call Monika. I resolved to share in the darkness which Kaspar had known for so many years. I held onto my woolly lamb and closed my eyes.

11. Toil

Next morning I awoke to Ahwenda's singing. She had lit a candle and was sitting on my bed. She gave me a hug and I buried my face in her hair, hair that had that special Ahwenda scent.

I am going to stay with you today, Kell. Monika has given me the day off. She says she has to find another way to teach me. She added sadly, *I don't think I am doing too well. I suppose dancing is lot tougher than running.*

I looked at her with wide eyes, I just couldn't imagine Ahwenda doing anything less than wonderfully. But I knew what she meant. Monika was a hard taskmaster, I couldn't remember her giving me a single compliment for all my efforts in play-practice.

Ahwenda, will you tell me a fairytale?

She smiled at me, *I will tell you about the Malachite Maid.*

Monika told Ahwenda they would have to start everything from scratch and go very, very slowly.

About a week later as the three of us were drinking herb tea, Monika stood up and left to fetch water. Ahwenda muttered, *I am so tired. I feel as though I have run miles and miles. And we've only practised for about an hour and a half.*

When Monika came back in we were lying on her couch on the verge of falling asleep. She glanced down at us with that inscrutable Monika expression and as she put the earthenware jug of water on the table asked if we were tired.

I'm exhausted, sighed Ahwenda.

Monika was warming her hands by the stove as she spoke, *Good, tiredness is a sign that you are learning at last. As for you, Kell, I am looking forward to the time when you are seven and we can begin to work in earnest.*

It was probably a good thing Monika didn't have slaves.

Ahwenda became ever more tired. She sometimes fell asleep in the afternoons just as I had got her to tell me a story. When this happened I just cuddled up beside her and lay there snugly daydreaming myself into fairytales where I would be rescuing princesses, unless Monika came and found me some chores to do. When Ahwenda woke she would moan that her whole body was writhing, twisting and turning even though she hadn't been moving her muscles at all.

One day shortly before Advent Ahwenda didn't come into my room to wake me. When I went into them, I saw her lying on the bed, Monika beside her dabbing her forehead with a wet cloth. Many days seemed to go by with Ahwenda burning with fever, hovering between sleep and dream, and hardly eating.

Late one night I got up and stumbled out of my little shelter, my fingers and feet were numb with cold my head beginning to spin as I tried to knock on Monika's door. I think I fainted. When I came round Miss was licking my face, Djorki barking, Monika was in her nightdress staring down at me, *Not you too, Kell.*

She lifted me and lay me on a sheep-skin near the stove. Ahwenda was burning, I was violently shivering.

About two more weeks went by until the time of the Winter solstice when more or less simultaneously her fever finally broke and my illness let go of me.

We had stayed in Monika's room, she had tended us day and night, and looked thoroughly exhausted herself. I have vague memories of Djorki and the cats often being with us.

We were too weak to attend the celebrations but Monika had a Yuletide tree brought in for us.

Something seemed to have changed between us all. Monika genuinely smiled and had an air of contentment about her when we were all together. Often she would just take Ahwenda's hand and mine in hers for no particular purpose except to hold us, to register that we were there with her. When she did this I usually reached out to Ahwenda so we could all hold hands together.

Why did we fall ill, I asked Monika as we were having breakfast one morning in early January.

I am wise enough to know that there is much I do not know. But one thing is clear your, she paused, *Our relation is deep. What with you freezing and Ahwenda boiling, and me trying to hold onto you both*, She gazed out of the window and sighed, *And there is one more.*

One more? I echoed.

In good time, Kell, she stood up, *We must get you washed and dressed, and back to play-practice.*

12. Ahwenda Misbehaving

We noticed the days beginning to lengthen and that magical Scandinavian light playing upon the snow-clad hillsides and in the village. Ahwenda was not allowed to practise dancing more than twice a day and then only for half an hour at a time. But she was still exhausted after every practice session.

This troubled me. I was worried about her and asked Monika if Ahwenda was well.

As well as can be expected, she replied in typical Monika fashion.

Did the illness take so much out of her?

No, it cleansed her.

But she washes every day.

Monika looked down at me with an odd expression then she shocked me, she actually exploded into laughter and didn't stop. *Oh Kell, Kell, if only you knew what eurythmy does to your etheric. Ahwenda is exhausted because she can do it. Those who can't do it, can play-act that they are dancing for hours. When Ahwenda does eurythmy her etheric is illumined but her body can't keep up, it sighs after the ethereal life forces and flakes out. But*, she stood up and I knew I was going to be fobbed off if I didn't react real quick.

Is that why she is a messenger, is that why she can run so swiftly?

She sat down again, *Yes Kell, that is why.*

I was beginning to learn that she would tell me lots of things if I could but find the right way to ask. I continued before she could change the subject, *I heard some men in the village saying that women were weak, that they couldn't run and that men were quicker, stronger and smarter than women.*

Dogs are quicker, stronger, a lot smarter and smell better than most of the men in this hamlet. But it is more complex. Solzhenitsyn spoke of a woman in the Gulag who could spend a whole day swinging from the hips and lifting bricks two at a time. None of the men could have done that but she could do it hour after hour after hour, day after day. Her etheric life forces were moving her body, her etheric was so much stronger than the men's. If she had not been incarcerated in the prison camp she may have become a world famous sportswoman. She shook her head sadly, *How many saw their hopes rubbed out in the camps of the Gulag?*

Before I had time to ask her what the Gulag was, she went on, *Men and women have different and complementary strengths. Men have more robust bodies, more physical strength and, if awake, they are more steadfast in their selves. Women have more life in their etheric and starry music in their astral.*

Astral?

She had already got up from the table, *Play-practice! Take out your balls out, the woollen ones.*

Monik–

Silence, play-practice!

She began to throw the balls at me, to the right, to the left, up, down, quicker, slower as I stood there trying to catch them.

After about five minutes she stopped, *That's enough for today.*

But that was great fun, can't we do it some more?

Without further word she took the balls and placed them back in the draw.

For the rest of the day your play-practice is to play.

I was on my way out when she added, *Thank you, Kell.*

For what?!

For reminding me that Ahwenda is still dancing too much. I shall have to cut it down to twenty minutes twice a day. As Stoner tells us, "Today rhythm replaces strength".

Eh?

Off you go!

I had learnt a lot. I had learnt there was something called the etheric, that etheric life forces move the physical body; that Ahwenda got so tired because her body couldn't keep up with her etheric; that there was something called the 'astral' which might have something to do with stars or with music. And there was the Gulag. It was just a matter of finding the right way and the right moment to ask her.

As I crunched through the snow I saw Moppar creeping toward Dungbjorn's dog which was digging with its front paws. The cat closed in, crouched rock still then suddenly with three bounds he was right behind the dog lashing its ass with his claws. The mutt squealed and raced off. Miss miaowed and ran over to me with her tail in the air.

With Ahwenda's dancing reduced to two sessions of twenty minutes each, one in the morning, one in the afternoon, we were able to spend a lot of time together. One time after lunch as we held hands walking in the snow covering the village, I asked her about the etheric and the astral. She frowned as she looked down at me, *The Grey and Monika are your teachers not me, you must wait for them to bring you insight.*

About the Gulag though she was more forthcoming. She explained how millions and millions had been interned in Russian concentration camps in the middle part of the twentieth century. She also told me that the Grey had taken her to see the woman who lifted bricks. How as a child she had stood with the Grey watching the woman in the actual history itself, how later, in her own imagining of that same scene, she had lived with the woman's tireless motion and how for a time her play-practice had been to emulate the woman. Ahwenda had gradually learnt to send the woman's loping, swinging movement down into her own legs so as to be able to run with her physical limbs carried in a tireless rhythm. *Even to this day on a hard day's run I picture to myself that woman's movements. A deep gratitude springs up in me as I reconnect with what she achieved in the Camps. The Grey One says that no matter whether people know about her or not, her deeds stand in the memory of the world ... for all to find who seek. He also told me that in the Gulag impulses from Heaven were locked in combat with those from below the earth. He has shown me many things in those camps, Kell.*

She shivered as though seeing in her mind's eye images of suffering Zaks, as those imprisoned in the Camps were called.

Once I teased her about how she would soon be able to make fire or break bones.

Don't be silly, Kell, eurythmy isn't about that. It's about making speech through movements.

'Tis not, it's about sprouting fire and breaking – wow, I bet Monika could crack rocks!

No Kell, she has learnt to speak in her dancing. Though her dancing she can speak to the nature beings, it is not her but the fire elementals hearkening to her gestures that make the fire, she only guides them through her movements. We might say, her gestures are speech for them.

What are elementals?

Ahwenda looked as though she had done something amiss, her beautiful blue-green eyes expressed an anxiety as she glanced over at Monika's dwelling. Then she swivelled, plucked a pile of fresh snow from a branch, dumped it on my head and ran off laughing. I ran after her, made a snowball, threw it at her and missed, made another … the snowball fight was great fun until I caught one of hers … on my nose.

I spent a lot of time watching the cats and tried to copy their way of creeping up on prey. I learnt to be stealthy. Once I crept up behind the last building before the rosy archway and came across Ahwenda. She was standing on one leg and making movements with her other foot in the air. Strange, subtle, slow, quick and fascinating movements. I sneaked right up behind her.

Kell, I, er – what are you up to?

Nothing, I was just watching you.

Sneaking up on me, you were!

Was not!

She squinted down at me.

What were you doing, Ahwenda, it looked fascinating?

Did it? Well, I was doing dance with my foot. I was doing the gestures for "B" and for "O" and for "W". She made the movements one after the other.

Someone made a grunting noise behind us. We both twirled round. Monika looked furious. *What are you doing, young lady?*

If she had been looking at me like that I would feel pretty certain I'd be taken to the bathing hut for a good scrubbing.

I was, I was – Ahwenda had gone red in the face.

I know what you were doing! Eurythmy with the legs is far more intense than with the arms – and I have been doing my best to stop you overtaxing yourself, but you have– she stopped in mid-sentence, *Kell, go to the bathing hut and see if there is warm water.*

It was like I thought, Ahwenda was surely in for a scrubbing down.

Actually it was me in for a bath. When I got back to Monika's they were drinking tea – real delicious black tea. Ahwenda bore a look of relief. She sprang up when I came in and threw me up in the air. Djorki had been lying by the stove, he jumped up and barked. Monika swivelled round and glared at him. The dog lay down again putting his head between his paws and trying, unsuccessfully, to look small. Ahwenda bowed her head meekly and went back to her tea but she gave me a wink as she sat down.

I don't think Ahwenda's misdemeanours went further than blurting out about elementals when she shouldn't or secretly practising dance when she oughtn't.

13. Vacating

The snow still remained, the nights were still very cold but the sun shone brightly and water was dripping from the roof tops and trickling in the beck. I was nearly six. The short compressed Spring was near.

One day as I stood watching water flowing in a rill, Monika came and stood beside me. *Kell*, her voice sounded distant as though her mind were somewhere else, *Spring is upon us*. She stood for some time before speaking again, *Ahwenda has exerted herself so much she needs a vacation*.

That would be good, as soon as I said it though I knew it wasn't good at all, it would mean she would be leaving. I blurted out, *I don't want her to go*.

Neither do I, Kell, but she is a woman, life's tasks will take her far.

I could feel that numbing sense of loss reaching deep inside me. *But you never leave and you're grown up*.

I have things to do, Kell, things to do. She was already walking away.

I went to the rosy archway and stopped a few steps from it. Whether trying to recall the instant of awakening to myself, whether trying to summon courage to cross the threshold and leave the hamlet or whether just waiting for that time when I too would be old enough to leave, I do not know. I stood there for a long time, for a long, long time for one who is not yet six. Till Miss and Moppar came to me and began weaving in and out between my legs purring loudly. They at least would be staying with me.

The day was set. Ahwenda was to leave the day after the morrow. That night it was she who stood at the open panel singing to me, singing the songs of Russia, of endless, endless forests.

When morning came I didn't want to get up. I wanted to sleep for a hundred years. Ahwenda brought me tea, real hot black tea from India but still I wouldn't get up or speak to her.

She left. My eyes filled with tears. I drifted in and out of sleep.

Kell, Kell, Ahwenda had removed the oak panel and was calling to me. *Aren't you getting up?*

No!

There's someone to see you.

I don't care.

He says, Kasparian knights don't sleep away the day.

I was up in a trice and opening the door. He was on the threshold, I hardly had time to mumble, *Grey,* before he had clasped me in his arms and was carrying me into Monika's for a late breakfast.

That day, the day before Ahwenda left, seemed to last a lifetime. The Grey One's presence brought a kind of duration to the passing moments. We laughed, sang, spoke of the days since we had parted, and thought in silence about the days to come.

As always he slept on the floor of my little dwelling. I slept long and deep. And when I woke he took me to see Kaspar.

This time Kaspar had been taken from the family that had first taken care of him. He was with a hard pedantic schoolmaster who had no love for the young man.

Thus do they seek to shutter his life anew. But they cannot succeed. Soon they will play their last card. The Grey's face was grim and determined as he spoke but sorrow lay in his eyes. Kaspar will live and die, and sacrifice his life to the full.

As the preparations for their departure were being made, I found myself thinking of Kaspar and wondering about the remainder of his short life … and how he was to die.

The Grey One would be accompanying Ahwenda, he stood beside me just before they left and spoke in a low voice, *Remember Kaspar, who had no visitors, no Monika, no Ahwenda, no Djorki, no Miss or Moppar. Just his little wooden horse as the years passed in voiceless darkness and he grew from a little boy to a teenager and on toward manhood.*

Ahwenda was close enough to hear, tears were rolling down her cheeks. For her too the high ideal of Kasparian knighthood had been presented.

14. The Empty Bed

The snow was rapidly melting. As they disappeared into the distance I felt not so much loss as a renewed longing to live as a Kasparian knight. I walked away from Monika and unlatched the door of my little room. I pretended to be entering a space of darkness. With closed eyes I felt my way to the bed and sat down on it, imagining I was in a closet no bigger than Kaspar's. I felt around until I put my hand on my woolly lamb and clasped it to my breast. And there I sat until my head began to nod and I lay down and slept.

When I woke, I was not quite sure where I was. I blinked my eyes and gazed around. Something was different. There was a second bed in my room. I went over to it, looked at it and wondered.

Then I ran into Monika. She was sitting gazing into the flames.

There is a second bed in my room.

I know.

Who put it there?

The Grey One said, it should go there.

Why?

Ask the Grey.

Is he going to sleep in it? It looks small.

Ask the Grey.

But he said, I should live alone in memory of Kaspar Hauser. So why is it there?

Ask the Grey One.

She stood up, I knew I would get nothing else out of her.

Next morning as soon as I woke, I glanced down to see if the bed were still there. It was. And once more I started to wonder about it.

Not more than a few days passed before he came back. My first question was about the second bed. He just smiled, *Can't an old man have his little surprise? But it is time we had some long talks you and I, about geography, history, many things*.

He told me about Russia and about the vast slumbering heart of the Slavic nations. I glimpsed how right up into the nineteenth century Russian families would lay the table for the unexpected guest. I saw a dwelling on the steppes, the evening meal was being served in the light of an oil lamp, an extra place had been set for the one who might suddenly appear. This same custom was always observed whenever the table was laid for the communal meal in our hamlet. The Grey One told me that much of what had lived in Russia and in other Slavic nations, is alive today in our own practices, in the lives of we who wait and prepare.

Once at Thursday's High Meal two Rangemen appeared bringing important news. Two extra plates and cutlery were brought in. The Rangemen ate quickly. At their side the empty place was laid and waited for another. I wondered about this and asked the Grey. The sad and the serious mingled with joy in his expression, almost as if he were reliving one of his own most poignant memories, as he answered, *The place is kept open always for Him. But ask no more now.*

More questions were coming out of my mouth but he put his forefinger gently to my lips.

He showed me an impoverished Russian pilgrim with a withered arm who wandered across the vastness of his country constantly repeating the Prayer of the Heart. And I saw that there were many, so very many who lived in this way.

With a sweep of his arm we seemed to move up into the

clouds and descend into a finely furnished room. Falarchs – he told me later they were Falarchs from Western and Central Europe – were discussing how to rip out the spiritual heart of Holy Russia and turn her, as one of them said with an effeminate giggle, into a 'Red Desert for Social Experiment'.

All at once the Falarch turned toward me, his face distorting into a leering, beckoning expression. The Grey put forth his hand in a gesture to hold back – and we were once again in the hamlet.

A most dangerous Falarch! Was his only comment.

Next day he brought me a vision of Revolutionary Terror. We were looking down upon Russia as from a great height, symbolically we saw dark eruptions bubbling over innumerable points of starlight on the landscape of Holy Russia.

Then we descended and I knew, I don't know how, that some years had passed. We were witness to tens of thousands of real men and women being marched into the prison camps, the Gulag.

This transformed into yet another vision. I saw hundreds of thousands of flowers each with a gleaming jewel growing upon the hardened lava of the dark eruptions, at those very places where points of starlight had once shone.

Just before he blew out the candle and left me to sleep with my woolly lamb, I asked him about this last vision.

Thus does goodness grow forth from suffering. Innumerable are the blue flowers with starlit jewels. And each has grown from a bed where pain has been patiently borne.

He blew out the candle and I lay in the dark, determined in my mind to visit a six year old Kaspar alone in his closet.

Next day, the day before he was to depart, the Grey One walked all around the hamlet with me. He did not speak and each time I tried to say something he made a gesture for me to be silent. We came to the archway. Buds of red and white rose were breaking forth in colour.

At last he spoke, *Little one, there is much that one knows and much, much more that one does not. There is a path we could walk together you and I but I am unsure if you can bear it yet*. He fell silent. I knew he was waiting for me to speak.

Where will the path take us?

Further into the way of Kaspar Hauser.

I wanted to say yes, but felt or saw, or felt I saw, a dark cavern before me. As I looked, the darkness of the cave became a chasm before my feet. I felt myself wobbling at the brink and looked up to the Grey One in a state of consternation.

You do not have to walk this way today. It can wait until you are older.

Inwardly I was still wobbling. It would have been so easy to turn back but part of me yearned to be a knight, longed to be able to fly across the chasm on a shining white stallion. Something steadied inside me, *Kaspar bore his suffering for all of us, didn't he?*

Yes, he did.

Then I will walk further with you into the way of Kaspar Hauser.

The Grey One nodded and gave me an encouraging smile.

After we had taken a simple meal, we returned to the rosy arch, this time to its very threshold. As he took my hand we were in another country, in another time. A man was riding a horse up to a country manner house. We entered the house, men were leaving the dinner table and going to a smoking room. The man, I had seen riding the horse, went with them. He looked anxious. Somehow I knew that he was an English Lord, that he was in debt and that they were prepared to pay his debts but at a price. I saw that they were explaining what he was expected to do. *It's just a little matter of taking a country bumpkin in tow and providing him with an, em, appropriate education*.

I saw he knew that it was far more than this but the other men spoke so convincingly, so encouragingly and yet with an undertone of threat in their voices that the English Lord acceded to their request. One of the other men laughed, *And they call him the Child of Europe!*

With a shock I grasped that they were speaking about Kaspar and that this English Lord had been chosen as the man who would take Kaspar away from the family he had been staying with and from the friends who loved him. My heart chilled as I realised this was a meeting of the False Architects. At the very moment of this insight, distortion entered into the scene. The faces of the Falarchs all turned toward me, they stood up, leering and advancing. I turned to the Grey One expecting him to block their advance. He did not move. Almost as if in memory I heard his voice say, as so often before, *Remember Kaspar*. And I felt rather than saw Kaspar in his prison, his dark prison in the wall.

The Falarchs halted their approach but still stood reaching out to me, beckoning me to come to them. I was wobbling as though on the brink of a chasm before my feet. All at once someone took hold of my hand, it was a child's hand which held mine, a boy of about my own age. He took his little wooden horse and placed it in my other hand. It shone brilliantly. The leering Falarchs fell back from its light. And we were again in the room of their meeting.

The men were congratulating the English Lord slapping

his back and giving him a large glass of sherry.

Thus does he try to wash away the blackness of his conscience with wine, as the Grey One spoke, we were back in the hamlet standing beneath the archway of roses.

They have no power to alter the memory of the world. But he or she, who would observe what the False Planners sought to achieve, needs the heart of a lion and great strength of purpose or else Falarchs will approach and strive to take hold of one who witnesses what they did in their richly furnished back rooms. You did well, little one, I– he stopped in mid-sentence, *Monika would be very proud.*

That was a compliment indeed.

As we were about to enter Monika's home he glanced down at me with a knowing smile and said, *They who take the trouble to visit Kaspar in his need, may find that he visits them in theirs*.

15. Maria

Next day, the day of departure, Ahwenda arrived. Her visit would be short for she would be accompanying the Grey One and their journey would be long. She was walking around the perimeter of the hamlet. I joined her. We paused before each of the five gateways. When we finally came to the rosy arch she spoke, *My time as a messenger, as a kind of raven for the Rangemen is drawing to a close, Kell. I am to begin another long apprenticeship*. A note of anxiety sounded in her voice.

Are you happy, Ahwenda, are you glad to be moving on?

She lowered her head, *I don't know. Yes, yes, I want to move on and to learn more about the way of Kasparian knighthood. But I have been happy with the Rangemen as never before in my life. And there is much that I love which will have to be left behind*. She fell silent.

Raynor, I whispered.

Her blue-green eyes glanced down keenly at me, *Him most of all*.

The problem of the empty bed had been constantly bugging me. Although I knew I wouldn't get the answer unless I was able to guess it first, I kept on asking him, at least once a day, why it was there. He had taken to giving me the same answer, *You never know when an unexpected guest might arrive*.

After learning about Russia I thought I knew the answer, the obvious one. As they were about to depart I said to him in a grown up sort of voice, *The bed is just like the empty place set at the table for one who might suddenly arrive, isn't it?*

He nodded solemnly, *It might be*, then his expression

turned to merriment, *And then again it might not.*

He turned to Monika, she was smirking so much she had to turn away. They know something I don't, I thought to myself.

The Grey spoke to her, *We mustn't make the lad grow up too quickly, let him play this Summer.* He ruffled my hair, stooped to kiss me on the forehead and added in a voice hardly above a whisper, *When I return, I may have a present for you.*

He looked pointedly at Ahwenda, she sprang away and ran swiftly as a deer though no animal could have run as gracefully. The Grey was beside her, his legs hardly seemed to be moving yet he was eating up the ground. Monika was gazing at them with a vague wistful smile. Djorki barked and set off in pursuit. He went a couple of hundred paces but wasn't able to close on them. Monika put her hands to her lips and called the dog back. I suddenly felt very tired almost as though I had been running beside them.

When the Grey One had shown me the slumbering spirituality of Holy Russia, the sufferings of the Gulag and the smarmy immoral machinations of the Falarch planners, it was almost as if my grown-up self drew into me. Yet as Spring lightened into Summer, as insects buzzed and the scent of flowers wafted through the air, and as we lost sight of the stars, it was as though those embryonic adult stirrings fell back to sleep. Even play-practice was stopped. Travellers were few. Djorki and the cats were constantly with me except when I slept alone as always. Every night I would imagine visiting Kaspar. And every morning as soon as I opened my eyes I looked down at the empty bed, and wondered.

Then came the morning, *the* morning. I awoke and

glanced at the bed, there was something different about it. I rose very quietly and went to it. The bedclothes were crumpled up. A mop of dark wavy hair stuck out from under them. Suddenly two small hands stretched up. She freed her face from the quilt and opened her eyes, very wide when caught sight of me. She sat up, pulled the bedclothes up to her neck and gazed back at me.

Who are you? I asked in German, I even used the polite form of speech.

For a moment she was silent then a torrent of words poured forth from her lips. I understood nothing but I knew she was speaking the language Monika sang to me in, Russian. She stopped speaking and smiled, her dark eyes upon me.

I was smiling too and spoke to her in English, *I am Kell.*

She pointed at herself, *Me, Maria.*

16. Summertime

Summertime, life was intense, wonderful but not easy. No, living was definitely not easy.

Monika came in to fetch both of us almost as soon as we started talking. Ahwenda and the Grey had brought Maria. We all ate breakfast together. We two children were always looking at each other, smiling and sometimes giggling. The grown ups stayed at the table after we had left it. Maybe they were giving us the chance to get to know each other. Maria spoke to me in Russian then realising I understood nothing she put her finger to her lip gazed into space and started again in English pronouncing the words very carefully and slowly, *You have my eyes*. I frowned not understanding what she meant. She repeated herself, *You have my eyes.*

I don't.

Yes, you do!

I do not.

You do.

I don't have your eyes, you've got your own eyes.

You do have them!

As she said this big tears came into her brown eyes. I felt both bad and startled. The grown ups had turned to look at us, Monika started to rise. Maria ran to her sobbing. Monika looked at me and said in a stern voice, *Kell?*

I threw myself on the floor crying bitterly. They must have let us both cry for a minute before Maria began speaking rapidly in Russian. Monika came over to me with Maria holding her hand, *Kell–*

I didn't let her finish, I jumped up and shouted, *She said, I'd got her eyes. But I don't have them, look at her*, I pointed at Maria, *I didn't steal her eyes!*

The Grey burst out laughing, Ahwenda did too. Monika looked over at them nonplussed for an instant then she too broke into laughter. Maria looked stricken, she cast herself on the floor and wailed. I was not to be outdone, I threw myself down again and started to bawl and sob. Maybe there was a kind of competition between us as to who could make the most noise.

Ahwenda came and sat between us taking one of Maria's hands and one of mine and speaking softly. Maria looked up at her. I looked at Ahwenda, *You speak Russian too.*

Better than any other language.

And Monika speaks it, I mumbled.

Better than any other language.

But I don't speak any Russian!

You will, Kell, I promise you, you will, said Monika.

Ahwenda continued to speak to Maria. All at once Maria burst out laughing and rained Russian back at her. Then she stopped and changed to English, *How do you say*, and there came a Russian word.

Mirror, said Ahwenda.

Mirror, repeated Maria and looked at me.

I shook my head, I didn't know the word in English. I knew, well sort of, what a mirror was because Monika had told me fairytales in which there were mirrors and even magic mirrors but in the hamlet there weren't any mirrors as far as I knew. People like Dungbjorn didn't care how they looked (nor how they smelled for that matter).

Maria leapt up and ran over to a little bag, pulled something out and hid it behind her back as she came over to me. She produced a mirror and showed me my face – which was a surprise. It was a big surprise to see myself. I had never seen myself except as a wavy reflection in water.

My eyes, your eyes, she said, *Let me show you.* She put her face beside mine and we looked into the mirror together. My eyes were not like the Grey's, nor Ahwenda's, nor Monika's, they were brown and so like, so very like Maria's.

I glanced over at Ahwenda and asked in Norwegian, *Is this a magic mirror?*

Maria looked at her inquisitively and she repeated what I'd said in Russian then they both burst out laughing. I felt tears coming up in me again. Ahwenda put her arm around me even as she was speaking in Russian to Maria, then she turned to the others and said in English, *We have to tell them.*

After exchanging a quick glance with the Grey, Monika said in English, *You do it.*

Ahwenda took my hand and took Maria's in her other and said in a prim and proper manner, *Kell and Maria, you are brother and sister.* She repeated this in German and then in Russian.

I could see this was a big surprise for Maria as well as me. All at once my sister cast herself into my chest, held onto me tightly and said in English, *I love you.*

I loved the Grey without realising it. I took Monika for granted yet I guess I loved her too. I loved Ahwenda, maybe I was a bit or more than a bit in love with her without really knowing it. But I loved Maria and I knew that I loved her.

She could come closer to me than anyone. She could make me laugh, she could make me cross, she could make me lose my temper, she could make me cry. She could make me despair, rage, cry and laugh all at the same time.

Today as I look back on those nine or ten weeks when we first met, I think I must have affected her in a similar way too. Our time together was so intense. It was as though twenty years of brother and sister tiffs, miffs, fun, tears and togetherness were telescoped into little more than two months.

We could laugh and cry, shout at each other, run away and complain to Monika about the other all in the space of a few minutes.

Maria slept in the little bed in my room. The first thing I thought of when I woke was: Maria. We spent all day and everyday together. I told her about Kaspar. And about going into history with the Grey. I even told her about the Falarchs, when I did this she started shouting in Russian, I think she must have been giving them a good telling off.

In the beginning we tried to speak English together, mine was better than hers. But soon, I don't quite know how, I began to understand her Russian so we spoke a mixture of English and Russian.

She was more of a fighter than me. I felt both her punches and her kicks, and though I wasn't above giving her a hefty shove I never hit her. She was more daring than me too. After I had told her about coming to myself in the wilds, she insisted on me taking her to – and through – the rosy arch.

Just after we had gone under the arch I heard Djorki barking. Looking back I have a suspicion that Monika had him keep and eye on us. As we turned to look at him I saw a big black mosquito settle on Maria's neck. I took a swipe at it. Suddenly we were surrounded by the gnats swishing at them with our hands even as we were running back to the arching roses. The moment we came through the archway the gnats retreated back to the wilds. Maria turned and shouted at them in Russian, probably in what adults call expletives.

I didn't turn back for I saw Monika striding toward us

and she didn't look at all pleased. She said something sharply in Russian, Maria turned to her and went red. Monika took us by the hand and marched us away. I knew where we were going even if my sister didn't. In spite of the gnat bites we were in for a good scrubbing in the Washing Hut.

17. Of Seeing and Not Seeing

Although I was so much together with Maria that little else seemed to matter to me, I couldn't help but notice that Monika began to look, well, happy. It was almost as though the face she had shown to the world for so long was but a mask, a mask starting to dissolve. I also noticed that she couldn't keep her eyes off Maria. She would just stand looking at her with a vague smile on her face.

The thought came to me that she loved Maria more than she loved me. And this cut me, cut me more, much more than when a similar notion came to me about Ahwenda. Maybe just because Maria was so close to me an odd element of competitiveness rose up. But I resolved to be brave and ask.

Maria had gone off to pick few herbs, Djorki was with her. Monika stood gazing at them as Maria danced about the dog which began barking wildly.

Monika?

Mm.

You love Maria more than me don't you?

Oh Kell!

I could see how pained she looked. She took my hand and started to walk away. At first I thought we might be going to the Washing Hut but we walked on toward the gateway of red and white roses.

Kell, please don't say that, don't even think it. Your mother died shortly after your sister was born. She is a year and a half younger than you. At that time there was a crisis. We did not, could not dare to risk you being taken together. She went silent.

Why couldn't we have grown up together?

Has the Grey given you insight into Falarch planning?

I nodded.

We feared that they had got word of you both and were seeking for you. If you had stayed together it would have been easier for them to locate you, she gazed out through the archway, they have their methods. And we might not have been able to defend you. You had to be separated. Maria was too young to travel. The Grey brought you here to this hamlet and soon after I came to take care of you. I was to take care of you, you Kell. Others took care of Maria in a place even I do not know. Things have gotten, or seem to have gotten easier lately so we decided to risk you being together – for a while at least.

All these years, Kell, when you could have grown up with your sister and I could have been with you both ... when I look at her I sense the joy that might have been had we all lived together. But no more now.

Her speech eased my heart.

At least it did until I was lying in my bed that same evening listening to my sister breathing and dreaming in her sleep, and I recalled that Monika had said "for a while at least". I shivered and held tightly to my woolly lamb, and tried to think of Kaspar alone in that pitch black space.

One obvious difference between me and my sister was that she spoke at least seven and probably ten words to every one of mine. This might explain why I soon began to understand her Russian, after a month I could grasp almost everything she said. And then I realised something strange. I became aware that often when she was speaking to me she would also be talking to herself. Well, talking to someone or something not there, so she was, as we would say, talking to herself.

Once I challenged her about this.

She replied simply, *I am talking to the elementals, the nature spirits, don't you see them?*

This led to our biggest crisis.

I said it was not true, that she was only pretending. She said, she wasn't. In the end I said she was lying. She screamed at me using a load of Russian words I didn't know. We both raced off to Monika complaining bitterly about each other.

Monika separated us for the rest of the day. Maria had Djorki. I had Miss and Moppar.

That night was bad. Maria stayed with Monika. I lay alone and couldn't sleep. Not even thinking about Kaspar allowed sleep to steal over me. At some point though I must have drifted into a dream.

Kaspar was with me, he was about my age or maybe a little older. We were both dressed alike in dark blue garments. He spoke to me. Even in the dream that felt odd because Kaspar never spoke.

What is troubling you, he asked.

My sister tells lies.

How do you know she is lying?

Because she speaks to things that aren't there.

How do you know they aren't there?

Because I can't see them! I felt very proud as I said this as if I had won an argument. *So Maria must be lying. I can be generous though, I can say she is just pretending*. I stepped up onto a stool so I stood head and shoulders above him.

He bowed his head and spoke very quietly, *Are things only there when you can see them?*

The stool seemed to sink from underneath me. I was standing on his level as he added, *When I was alone in the darkness, did the world not exist because I could not see it?*

The ground seemed to descend under my feet so that I stood looking up at him. I wanted to say something but couldn't think of anything to say. My head was about on a level with his knees.

Does she really see things that I can't?

He did not speak at once, he just looked at me, then he posed another question, *Do you love her?*

At this point the dream disappeared, I was woken by Monika who came in carrying my sister, *She has been crying all night and wanted to come in to you.*

Maria reached out to me. Monika slipped her under my quilt, my sister clung onto me. I wanted to say that I believed her or would at least try to believe her. All I said though was, *I love you*, in Russian.

She mumbled something and fell asleep almost at once. Monika drew the heavy curtains, lit a candle and set herself in the chair. I closed my eyes wishing I could sleep too.

Kell?

I didn't answer.

Kell, I know you can hear me. Listen, listen to me, you have hurt her deeply.

I opened my eyes wide, *I know.*

But I do not blame you. It is hard, so very hard to believe in the hidden worlds.

Can she see them?

How deeply, how clearly, how consciously – that I cannot answer. But yes, she sees into the hidden ethereal.

Can you see the ethereal?

She blew out the candle. I was afraid she might get up and leave but she made no movement. I was almost asleep when she finally answered, *Yes, Kell, I can see the living ethers. I know how to enter and how to leave the sphere of living forces.*

Maria has much to learn. She has to know how to differentiate, that is, to know when to open her etheric sight and just as importantly when and how to close it off again. And she has to learn to be silent. The tone of her voice changed, if I could have seen more than her outline in the darkness I think she would have been smiling as she added, *And learning to be silent, I fear, will be a lot harder for her than for you.*

Monika?

Yes?

Will you teach me to see the etheric?

I can teach you to prepare for the time when, she paused as if trying to find the right words, *for the moment when Life herself opens your etheric vision*.

I was fully awake now and hoping we could continue to talk and not stop abruptly. I lay looking in her direction.

Are you afraid of the dark, Kell?

No, I just think of Kaspar alone without light and then I am not afraid. The tone of my voice surprised me, it sounded more grown up than I felt.

Good, I think I shall say more. There is a magic age, well, there are many ages of magical renewal, but for you the magic age of seven will arrive, Stoner spoke openly of this. For some it comes sooner, for others a bit later than their seventh birthday. At this time part of your etheric forces are released. And it becomes possible to train these freed etheric life forces. Before this period your etheric forces are fully active in remaking your own body. The body you receive from your parents is not truly your own, you have to make it yours. Only then can this surplus of living forces be released for schooling. If we seek to work with the etheric before this time, we risk taking these forces away from the rebuilding of your own body and this can seriously undermine your health and well-being later in life. That is why I say to you again and again, "All in good time, Kell, all in good time".

But Maria isn't seven and she can see the etheric, she can see – what did you call them?

Elemental beings

Yes.

Some few are born with this sight. Yet most lose it quickly and forget. Some keep the vision either because they are handicapped or–

Is Maria handicapped? I felt stricken as I said that.

I could hear her laughing quietly to herself before she answered, *Well, she does talk rather a lot but otherwise nothing is wrong with her.*

I put my arms around my sister and squeezed her. She moaned slightly. I felt a strain inside me release itself.

Monika can the Grey One see the etheric?

What can he not see? The etheric, the astral, the higher heavenly realms.

The astral? As I said it, I knew at once I'd overstepped, I could almost sense her tensing as if about to rise with an abrupt "Good night". I had to react quickly, *All in good time, eh Monika, all in good time.*

Oh Kell, you are starting to learn – at last!

I decided to risk another question. *Can you see into the higher heavenly realms?*

There was a tension in the room but a different kind of tension, she was very quiet for some moments before answering, *Yes*, then she added, *Yes and no, how can I explain?*

She stood up as she spoke, *The Empty Mountain says that to live without love is to live in hell – and to enter the regions of eternity without love is to enter into eternal hell. I have been wounded, Kell, badly wounded. If you seek to enter the heavenly worlds without being willing to forgive, you bring something dark to both heaven and earth. I am in a state of convalescence. Once I could enter and, who knows, maybe again ... but of this, Kell, and listen to me very, very carefully, I will not speak so don't ask, don't dare to ask!*

I am not sure I understood anything about what she was telling me but I did know she had tried to answer my question and that was enough. I also felt very sleepy. Maria murmured in her sleep and turned over. I wondered if she had been listening to us from the place where she was in sleep. A last question came to me, I wanted to ask if Maria had more insight, greater qualities, more talent than than me. All I said was though, *Maria is better than me, isn't she?*

I could sense Monika move toward me, she put her hand to my hair and caressed it, *Kell, my Kell, you have your own talents different from those of your sister. Though few indeed can measure themselves with her.*

Will she be a Kasparian knight?

Maybe a Sophianic seeress.

A what?

No more now! I will only say this before I say goodnight, what you two can achieve together can be far greater than what either of you might achieve alone.

As she opened the door she added, *Take good care of your sister.*

I kissed Maria on the forehead, she murmured again and gave me a shove.

18. Being Properly Presented

When I woke I reached out for my sister, she wasn't there. All the events of yesterday came rushing back to me. I glanced down at the other bed, it was empty. I ran out without getting fully dressed and into Monika. Maria was sitting at the table, she didn't seem to have touched the food in front of her. She gave me an unreadable look. I suddenly felt very shy but went to sit beside her. She picked up a piece of bread and gazed at her plate. Monika said she was going to fetch water and left us alone.

My sister sat very still looking down at her food.

Are you angry with me, Maria?

No. But she still kept her head lowered.

I didn't know what to say. In the end I said, *Won't you speak to me?*

Monika says, I talk too much.

Her eyes seemed to be about to bulge with tears but I felt like sunrise, I just wanted to hug and tease her though I did my best to keep from smiling and made my voice sound very serious, *I want you to tell me about elementals, I want to know about what happens in the hidden ethers*.

She turned to me with big wide open eyes, *Do you believe me?*

Yes, I believe you.

We had been speaking English. Suddenly she snapped over into Russian speaking with such rapidity that I hardly knew what she was saying, I was just listening to her voice and watching her animated expression and the sparkle in her eyes.

The door opened, Monika stepped over the threshold, Maria stopped dead, her cheeks went bright red. Monika had her stone face on but her lips stretched slightly and, as my sister looked down at her food, she gave me a wink.

Maria started coughing and choking on her bread.

We went outside a bit later. As Maria danced toward the flower beds I thought about the hidden world of ethereal life forces, about the nature spirits, about all that she could see that I couldn't. And I resolved that one day I too would be able to see that world.

It was about mid-morning when she broached the subject of the elemental beings, *They wanted me to tell you about them, Kell. They love you being here with them. They wanted me to tell you about them so you could acknowledge their presence.*

Djorki was lying a few yards from us, he gave a low growl. I looked up and saw Dungbjorn walking with his mutt which was keeping a very wary eye on our dog. After they had passed by she spoke again, *It's not like Monika thinks. I don't blab! I don't talk about nature spirits to, to*, she glanced at Dung just as he disappeared behind a building, *To, to the Dungbjorns of this world. I don't, I don't. But the elementals themselves kept asking me to tell you about their presence here.*

I put my finger to her lips. She looked at me in surprise.

Call them over, tell them I want, er, to be properly introduced.

She jumped up and ran around calling out strange words in whispers. Then she came back, walking very primly with her hands behind her back and stood beside me. She gestured with her hand, *They are here lined up before you.*

One by one she spoke their names, described how they looked, and had me reach out with my fingertip so they could touch it.

Another month went by, five, six weeks. We were always

together. And now we shared a secret about the nature spirits so we were no longer just little children, we were big little children. My Russian became more fluent. Our tiffs and misunderstandings became less, slightly less frequent.

The Grey and Ahwenda often came to visit us and when this happened Monika seemed so glad. She looked overjoyed as she watched me and my sister try to accomplish the impossible of touching Ahwenda in a game of tag.

Whenever the Grey One left, Ahwenda went with him.

19. Sneaking Off

So many and varied things we two experienced every day. Maria would tell me about what the elementals were up to when the winds swirled or when it rained. We roamed everywhere in the village. Only once did we get ourselves into real danger.

My sister was fascinated about where the cats went. She made up stories about them and even had me imagining that they had discovered the entrance to a secret underground cavern with rushing, tumbling streams and a clear still lake, caves and chambers where jewels and precious metals jutted from the rocky walls. So for a few days we tried to keep a wary eye on Miss and Moppar. Somehow though they always seemed to sneak off for an hour or two. My sister became more and more exasperated. Not even the elementals would tell her where the cats went.

One morning she got up and made me pledge that we would stick to the cats no matter what. The first hour or two went very, very slowly. The cats basked in the sun and slept. Then Moppar stretched, yawned and walked away. Miss followed him. Maria was clinging to me almost shaking with excitement. The cats strolled around as though their only care was to decide where to lie down and take their next nap.

Moppar stopped, sniffed the air, his tail started wagging. Suddenly he was off running between bushes as though chasing something and Miss was after him, and Maria after her. I ran after them dodging around the bushes with a gathering sense of disorientation. I lost sight of the cats but could see Maria weaving between branches. I came running around a bush, she had stopped, I bumped into her sending her flying. She hit the ground, rolled over onto her back and sat up shouting at me in Russian. She must have been uttering an expletive version of telling me I was a lout behaving loutishly.

Taken aback by the shock of knocking into her and the verbal battering from her lips, I stood with my mouth open but noticed Miss creeping on her belly, full of concentration as though stalking prey and crawling toward an exit from the hamlet. Maria must have seen something in my expression because she stopped her shouting and glanced back behind her just as Miss sprang forward and away.

My sister was on her feet scrambling after the cat. My voice was only a squeak as I tried to call her name but my feet were running after her. I grabbed her shoulder just before she reached the exit. She swivelled round taking my hand in both of hers, anger smouldering in her brown eyes. I sort of winced as though expecting a second round of fiery Russian expletives but I managed to get my words in first, *Maria, that's an entrance to the hamlet!*

She glanced over her shoulder at the two pillars of stone with the heavy stone cross-piece resting on them and threw my hand down as she spoke, *I'm going after the cats*.

But it's an entrance to the hamlet.

You like repeating yourself! She was giving me a challenging look.

But–

Are you afraid?

This was female logic. Even when I was a kid I was a sucker for female logic.

Her expression transformed into coy disgust as she lifted her chin and turned toward the stone threshold. I held her back by her upper arms, her body was straining against my grip.

All right, all right, but let me go first.

I had been totally undone by the feminine mode of conducting an argument.

Coming under the stone plinth of the entrance, I bowed my head and walked quickly and guiltily through. For three or four steps nothing seemed to change. My face brightened, I called her to follow me but as I turned toward her, a chill took away my breath and an icy coolness seemed to grip and spread through my limbs. She walked between the pillars with a queenly air then her expression also began to show anxiety.

I stood immobilised almost as though watching myself in a dream.

A soft hissing, a small black snake was slowly gliding toward me – and I couldn't seem to move. The snake came closer and lifted its head, its forked tongue flickering.

A noise in the grass, Moppar took the snake by its neck. I felt I could move again. But two similar black snakes were slithering toward my sister. I ran and kicked away one, Miss pounced on the other.

A bigger browny green snake slid across blocking our way back to the entrance. We backed away and began to run. Djorki barked.

We seemed unable to catch our breaths. Just as we stopped and turned back I noticed one of the black snakes to my left. Maria grabbed my arm and pointed to our right, another black snake was stirring in the grass. There were five or six snakes, we were encircled. The serpents seemed to be spiralling in toward us.

Djorki was barking wildly at the huge brown snake whose head was lifted and swaying. Monika appeared framed by the stone pillars and plinth. She stood perfectly still for a moment then made a cutting movement with her right hand. The snake fell lifeless.

Djorki was running toward us. Monika's call halted him. She seemed to be blowing and as she blew her hands made weaving motions. Warmth enveloped us. The black snakes began to glide away.

Djorki was panting beside us, Monika standing sternly in front of us. She didn't speak, she just pointed back toward the entrance of the hamlet.

I was holding my sister's hand as we went with bowed heads under the stone plinth. I felt so exhausted I could have gladly dropped to the ground and slept.

After we had come through the bushes I felt my sister pulling me toward our home. But I knew we would be making a detour. And this time I was actually looking forward to being scrubbed with hot water in the Washing Hut.

20. The Sun Darkens

One morning the dogs started barking wildly. We rushed out and saw the air filled with birds.

Carrion fowl, Monika muttered shaking her head.

That evening the Grey came with Ahwenda. Next morning half a dozen Rangemen appeared. There were hushed discussions. Monika's became a face of granite. Even the Grey One looked troubled. My heart was pierced with misgiving. For the first time neither I nor my sister were able to laugh. Heavy clouds covered the sky. A shadow seemed to spread over the hamlet.

After the evening meal the Grey and Ahwenda came to us at Monika's. None of us spoke. At last the Grey One broke the silence, *There are large movements of animals, wargs have been seen and scouts of the Hordes have been detected not many leagues distant. It is too dangerous for the three children to remain together.*

I am not a child! Ahwenda stood with her arms folded.

No, no. Nevertheless– he paused glancing over to Monika who sat crumpled on a chair with her gaze fixed on the wall, she looked like a little old woman, *Tomorrow I will depart with Ahwenda and Maria.*

Maria had slept beside me in my bed. We had spoken little, cried much. When I woke, she was not there. For a few desperate moments I thought they might have already taken her and left. As I dressed tears were rolling down my face.

The morning sky was still covered in low, unnaturally dark clouds. We were outside the hamlet my sister was holding my hand, we did not speak. Monika glanced pointedly at her, Maria slipped my hand and stood in front of me, *You are my brother, my only brother, no matter how long we are apart, I will always remember you, I will always love you.*

Her voice sounded very grown up. Years later she told me that Monika had woken her and begged her to give me a farewell I would remember. Having made her speech, her eyes filled with tears and she cast herself into my arms and cried, and cried. They finally had to pull us apart by force.

As the Grey One started to move away with my sister in his arms, Monika took a jewel and slipped it into her hand. I looked at them, I had given her nothing, I had nothing to give. Then suddenly I shouted, *Wait!* And ran, tumbled, got up and ran to my room.

I came back and put my woolly lamb into my sister's hands.

We stood waving until they were out of sight. Still we waited and did not speak. They were gone. I retreated to my room. Cried and slept. Slept and cried. The day passed. Next day I didn't get up. I was shivering and faint, feverish and mythered.

Losing Maria pierced me more deeply than any other loss. It was as if my very self were being torn apart. If part of me fell asleep whenever the Grey One departed, when Maria left, part of me died. And the part that remained only wanted to die.

The illness lasted a long time. For more than a month I was delirious. Sleep, dreaming, waking were no longer segregated – and something dark, dark and final, drew ever closer to me. I only wanted to disappear into sleep, into death-like slumber.

There came a time, I am told, when the sickness began to peak. My fever rose, they were unable to get me to eat, very little could I drink. But I remember a dream or maybe a vision. I stood on the shores of a misty Celtic mere. A boatman, hooded so that I could not see his face, beckoned to me. As I was about to set foot in his boat I turned back … and was pulled with extreme force into my body lying in the bed. Djorki was barking, Monika shouting at a Rangeman. I found out later it was Raynor.

Fetch him, go at once, don't dare return without him.

The Rangeman mumbled something inaudible.

She went on, *Wherever he is find him. He left us! It is beyond my power to preserve Kell. Go, go now and don't come back without him.*

Raynor told me years later that he had felt as if he were being beaten up. As he went forth from her door he vomited. He ran from the hamlet, not knowing where the Grey or Ahwenda were. He ran and ran, stumbled picked himself up, ran, ran and stumbled again and again, then he fell into a fever. He knew not where he was or where he was going. Ahwenda found him many days later in a little dwelling still very weak. Apparently someone had taken care of him after he fainted in the wilds but who it was he could never remember.

Of all this I knew nothing. As he left the door I was drawn once more back into the dream, I could hear the faint lapping of the water and though I could see nothing I knew I was at the lake. Ages seemed to pass as I waited there. Then I remember a voice calling to me. I opened my eyes, it was very dark.

Monika, I croaked.

She is sleeping, it was a man's voice, deep and resonant, *She needs sleep.*

I can't see you.

He made a rumbling sound which might have been laughter, *And do you believe I am not here, because you cannot see me?*

I know you are here.

Then I will bring a little light. A point of bluish light shone from somewhere, I do not know if it were near or very far away but as I looked, the source of light became more yellow, it became a lantern glowing on the table. I saw Monika lying as one dead upon the floor. He was young, tall, and seemed very strong.

Who are you?

I am one who cuts back wood, he gestured to a bundle of branches tied together and laid against the door, *And dissolves stones.*

Why are you here?

He didn't answer at once but came closer to me and sat on the floor. A fresh scent of blossom and resin wafted from his garments. *What ails you, little one?*

I have lost my sister.

He made a sweeping gesture with his right hand and I was back in the vision of the lake, one foot already in the boat. Behind me I heard his voice, faint but distinct. I turned and found myself back with him in the room. I understood that he had asked me if I wanted to find her.

Yes, I answered very weakly.

He arose and took from the bundle by the door a twig. I noticed a vase of water on the table. *I will give you a branch*, he said as he set it in the water, *And I will give you healing sleep.*

And I slept. For more than two days I slept. And Monika slept too. Djorki lay outside the door and would let no one enter. We awoke almost at the same instant. I heard, or thought I heard, Monika singing a Russian song. When I opened my eyes, she was still dead to the world upon the floor but as I looked she stirred and mumbled, *Did you call me, Kell?*

Upon the table the twig stood in the vase. Small white roses had flowered upon it but there were no thorns.

21. Wanderers Return

Advent was upon us before I was able to rise from my bed. I was still very weak as was Monika. We had lain together in her home, me in her bed, she on the sofa. Frequently not speaking for an hour or more at a time. Djorki and the cats had often been with us. One of the guards brought us meals. Otherwise no one visited us. The days were short. The nights very long.

At the end of each day as I felt sleep coming upon me, I would visit Kaspar, the Kaspar of my own age, in my mind. There was no fuss, I would enter into his little closet, he would move up a little so we could sit beside each other in the dark, the quiet darkness of his abode. He would put a little horse in my hand so that we both sat with a wooden horse as we waited. More and more I found that I loved the silent dark.

And I enjoyed being with Monika even when we were not talking just looking at the flames in the fire. I would look out of the window at the most silent stars and wait, and I knew I was alive.

At the Winter Solstice – around midnight of the longest night – there was an interruption. Dungbjorn had got his hands on strong drink. He was carousing, shouting, singing. One of the guards knocked on our door and explained that Dungbjorn and his followers had laid two of the guards low and were bragging they would take over the leadership of the hamlet.

Monika struggled up from her bed, *There is no peace for the wicked, Kell. The Dungbjorns of this world keep us on our toes*. But as she tried to stand she went faint and had to sit again. *I am still too weak*. She asked the guard to take Djorki instead. *Make him learn, my good dog, make him learn.*

The rumpus was over in a few moments. Djorki ran up at full pace and rammed his front paws into Dungbjorn's chest knocking him flat on his back. While the guards quickly dealt with the other drunkards, Djorki stood with his nose over Dungbjorn's crotch. Growling if he moved a muscle. It was about fifteen degrees below freezing point. After ten minutes Dungbjorn was crying and begging Monika to save him. She called from the window. Djorki bounded gladly back to us.

There were no more disturbances in the village that Winter.

I was still a little too weak to join in the Yuletide festivities but I began to get up and even go outside. The Grey One and Ahwenda returned one afternoon during the Holy Nights. Some Rangemen who had arrived a few hours earlier went with Ahwenda outside the hamlet. I was left with Monika and the Grey. She told me to go and play so she could have a cosy chat with him. I slipped very quietly into my little dwelling, stood on my bed and peered through a crack beside the connecting panel. They hadn't started a conversation.

Suddenly Monika said severely, *Why didn't you come?*

Monika–

Why didn't you come? Her voice was raised, *I called you, I sent for you. Kell was so ill, I thought he might die. Why didn't you come?*

He hung his head and spoke softly, *I was told to go elsewhere.*

Her voice exploded, *What do you mean, you were told to go elsewhere – you are the one who does the telling!*

In my imagination I pictured her pushing him outside and dragging him to the Washing Hut, stripping him and giving him a good scrubbing.

He looked at her sorrowfully and reached out to her as he spoke, *He said, he would come himself.*

Monika opened her mouth as if to bawl him out again but something must have struck her because she just said, *Oh!* with a stupid expression on her face. Then she turned to the table, *The twig, we threw it out!*

Shortly after Ahwenda burst into the room, *Raynor is missing!*

I saw Monika sway as though she might faint but she took the Grey by his arm and whispered, *Please find him, it was – oh, please find him.*

He nodded and without further word departed with Ahwenda.

They were away for three days. Monika hardly spoke and spent much of her time in the shrine. But they did succeed in finding Raynor and bringing him back to the village. Ahwenda found him but there is a secret to that story though.

Maria constantly wove in and out of my thoughts. Perhaps because of the illness, it was only at the end of the Holy Nights, as I was lying in the dark, that I came to a realisation: My sister had no Djorki, no Miss or Moppar, no Monika, she didn't have the Grey or Ahwenda; she was far away. I didn't know where she was or even if she had anyone to speak Russian to. In the darkness I called out to the Grey One, he must have been there sitting very still in my dwelling because he answered me straight away.

Where is Maria?

She is safe.

How do you know?

I know.

He was always able to comfort me. When he said, "I

know", I somehow knew that he did. *Does she have anyone to speak Russian to?*

Yes, she is with people who love her. She is not alone in the world.

Does she have any animals to play with?

From out of the darkness I felt his hand caress my hair, *She has a little woolly lamb*.

I thought of my little lamb and was glad she had it. I rolled over onto my side beginning to feel sleepy, *Will I be able to see her?*

Not soon, little one, crises are coming; we might even have to abandon this village.

Leave the hamlet? I shivered and pulled the quilt tightly around me.

22. Now We Are Seven

Now we are seven, she said.

But I thought you were a little bit older, Monika.

Now we are seven, we can begin to learn together.

Using freed etheric forces?

Get your balls!

I took out my woollen balls, there were eight now. She started throwing them at me rapidly one after another: up, down, left, right. I caught six of them fairly easily but fumbled one and didn't get my hands on the last ball at all.

Time for new balls and real throwing! Her eyes glinted with excitement as though she had been waiting for this moment for many years.

The balls for throwing were made of string wound into a tight ball and stitched so the string wouldn't easily fall apart. For the first practice she made me stand about five paces from an oak tree and showed me how to throw. Her movement was similar to a javelin thrower's though effortlessly relaxed and flowing. All I had to do was throw the string ball and hit the tree. She watched me try, corrected my movements, watched me for a couple more throws, nodded and said, *That's a start, Kell, keep practising*. Then she left me for an hour.

This began the first week's practice. It continued everyday: Throw the five string balls, one at a time, pick them up, throw them again ... one hour, two hours. It was all too easy and boring. I started imagining that the balls were knives and that the tree was a troll. I could picture its face in the bark. I tried to aim at its snout. Eventually I got a ball to strike the troll's nose and jumped up excitedly. I heard Monika's voice from behind me.

You are trying to aim too much. Time for new balls and

new techniques.

The next set of balls were more intricately made. Two pieces of wood, notched in the middle so that they could make a cross, were wound together with string into a tight ball, finally a leather cover was stitched around. Such a ball fitted nicely into my hand. Many hours of play-practice were used trying to make or mend them. I liked throwing more than notching, binding and stitching. And my attempts to make a ball or repair a damaged one invariably needed redoing. Monika was nothing if not patient but she wouldn't tolerate lack of effort. I'd be sent to cover earthen toilets or clean floors if she didn't think I was trying enough.

Once after trying to make a ball three times, and each time having her pull it apart and being told to begin again, I groaned, *Why can't we use stones instead of balls?*

Because, Kell, you have no idea what a stone is. Do you know when it was made, how it was made and who made it?

Nobody made it, it's just a stone.

No person made it, I grant you, but the rock came into being once ages long ago and of this you know nothing, so how can you make the stone yours? When you construct a ball yourself, you get to know it, you put yourself into it. It becomes in a sense an extension of yourself.

I had no answer for this but when I thought of the mending, winding, stitching and binding and how sore my fingers often were – I remained far from convinced.

Once she kept me away from throwing for three days, I just had to make and repair balls. And then I stubbornly refused to mend them any more. She quietly took away all my throwing items and told me that from now on mopping would be my play-practice. I held this out for two days until I was by myself supposedly mopping out the

Washing Hut but really imagining the mop to be a lance and the stream which flowed through the outer part of the hut to be fire pouring from the dragon's mouth. *Dragon, you will feel the steel of this magic lance*. I held the mop horizontally and was about to charge when I heard an em-sound. I swivelled round and saw her standing feet apart and arms folded.

Some knights are known as knight of the lance, others as knights of the sword. Perhaps you will become known as the knight with the mop.

That night I woke up in the middle of a vivid dream, one in which I had been much older than I was, a teenager growing into a young man clad in a knight's armour upon a white stallion. In the dream I had ridden proudly into an encampment of knights and their retinues, proclaiming loudly that I would enter their tournament. Squires and even younger boys rushed out of tents and goggled at me but I hardly deigned to glance down at them. I waited silently for the knights themselves to appear. The youngsters started to snigger. One of the boys stepped closer, pointing up at me, *Maybe his tactic will be to mop up diarrhoea and get the other combatants to pass out from the stench*.

The squires roared with laughter. I looked down at my lance. It was a mop.

They were calling to the knights, *Come, come and see the Knight with the Mop*.

A huge armoured knight strode out of a tent. A squire called out to him, *Careful, Sir Gwinafor, or the stink will cause you to keel over and he'll mop you up*.

Voices joined in to jeer me, *To arms, to arms, the Knight with the Mop is upon us!*

I awoke with their mocking laughter still sounding from the dream. It was cold, the darkness around me total.

Monika, I croaked.

There was no answer.

Usually if I woke in the night I only had to whisper her name and she would quickly remove the connecting panel. Three times I called, waiting a minute between each call. Then I let out a stifled shout. Soon I heard the noise of the panel being removed, candlelight flooded into my room.

Monika, I was sniffing and sobbing.

Yes.

Monika.

Yes.

Monika!

Kell.

Monika, I shouted out, *I don't want to be a knight with a mop.*

When the history of the world is tallied up, it might be found that mops have done greater deeds than swords.

Next day we returned to throwing. Ten paces from a silver birch. I had to throw and hit the tree trunk.

Smooth throwing, Kell, and remember to follow through.

Gradually my throwing improved. It became natural for me to let the ball fly with an arrow's line, to spin it, or to toss it into the air and let it fall onto a leaf half a dozen steps away. I hardly noticed how this improvement came about. Usually I was worse at the end of a practice session that at the beginning. Yet when I looked back over the weeks I could see real progress.

Monika said I did my best throwing when I was sound asleep in bed.

She would often set me a new task before I had really got the hang of the one before. The new tasks could be daunting. I'd practise for hours and hours, for days and days. And when it seemed I would never learn and came to her pleading for help, she would look at me and say, *Try – but don't try.*

Always the same answer.

She had set me a tough task. I had to throw one of the leathern balls at the trunk of a slender birch about ten grown-up paces away. She marked a circle for me to stand in, and half way between the birch and the circle she set a stave upright in the ground, only it was not quite in the direct line between them, it was a small step to the right. My task was to throw the ball to the right of this stake and make it swerve back to hit the trunk.

How can I do that? I asked incredulously.

You hold the ball with your hand relaxed but your fingertips gripping it tightly so when it's released it spins. If you do it in the right way it will swerve around the pole and hit the tree.

After days of practising I managed to get the ball to spin and swerve but nowhere near enough to bend it back into the tree trunk. One afternoon in anger I threw the ball as hard as I could into the pole. The ball split apart. Half a day would be needed to repair it. I kicked the ground in disgust and shouted, *Monika*.

She came from the hall where she had been dancing and crossed the ground swiftly, her cream-coloured silk gown blowing in the breeze.

It's impossible. I can't do it, I can't!

I thought she might get mad at me but she just beckoned and turned on her heel. I ran after her. She entered her home with me close behind, I reached out and touched the flowing silk folds of her dress. She gestured for me to sit at the table. As I sat down she pulled back a kind of curtain on a wall to reveal a picture of a conjurer with a wide-brimmed hat standing and doing tricks on a little table in front of him.

Look very carefully, having said that she took a kettle and started to make herb tea.

I sat there gazing at the picture and taking it in. The man in it, wasn't looking at what his hands were doing yet he had poise and certainty. (Many years later I learnt that this was her own coloured drawing of the Magician, the first arcanum of the Tarot de Marseilles.)

She placed two small cakes and two cups of tea on the table.

The Magician, she said casting a glance at the picture, *Learn from him how to turn work into play, how to make burdens light and yokes which bind you easy. That was written by Empty Mountain nearly a century and a half ago. I have always found the advice sound.*

My tea was laced with berry syrup. We ate and drank without speaking for a couple of minutes before she went on, *See the hat, like a figure of eight. Let's stand up and move a lemniscate.*

What's a lemniscate?

A figure of eight.

What's a figure of eight? I still didn't know numbers.

She wrinkled her nose and shook her head slightly then drew with her finger an eight on its side in the air. We moved it.

Don't pace it out with your feet, move with your heart, let your feet follow the movement of your chest. This is a repeating figure, a never-ending rhythm beating continually like the heart itself. She was about a yard away from me on my right, we moved smoothly together. We were still moving as she continued, *See the yellow circle of the hat like a sun around the head, like gold around the heads of medieval saints.*

What are they?

Her eyes narrowed, *You know about knights but not saints, I can see I shall soon have to tell you more than fairytales*. She pointed at the picture, *Look at the yellow circle, it is as though sunshine from the heart were streaming up to warm a cold calculating brow. Learn that craftiness needs to be silent before innocence*.

I wasn't following, I dropped my head and came out of the rhythm of the motion.

She knelt on one knee and took my hands, *Don't worry about what I'm saying, just look at the picture, take it in. Take it with you into your practising*.

Do you want me to take it down from the wall?

She stood up, a Slavic sternness settling again on her features, *You take it with you in your mind, you imagine him!*

Every time I started play-practice I tried to picture the Magician. It wasn't as easy for me as it might have seemed. Sometimes I could only get his hat and his face. Sometimes I had bits of him but couldn't put them together. Sometimes I saw him clearly – but when I looked again at the picture on the wall, I realised that mine didn't match Monika's drawing.

And yet over days, weeks … indeed over years and decades my inner picturing of the first arcanum became a friend and a blessing.

About a fortnight after she had shown me her picture I threw the ball, it almost clicked out of my fingers and spun rapidly around the stake to hit the side of the tree. *Monika*, I shouted jubilantly as I danced wildly around.

One of the villagers turned on me telling me to keep my voice down. When Monika came, I was so excited I could barely keep from jumping up and down, *I've done it, I can do it!*

Show me.

She was standing upright, unsmiling, arms folded. I picked up a leathern ball and tried to get it to 'click' out of my fingers. When I let it go, it just puffed up into the air and didn't even reach the stake.

Keep practising, Kell.

She was already walking away before I could open my mouth.

It took a couple of more days before that special zip came again as I let go of the ball and it swerved around the stave and back into the tree. I shouted her again though not quite as confidently as the first time. She came and stood by as I threw the ball. It flew in a straight line and missed the tree by about four paces.

Keep practising.

I didn't turn round to look at her, I knew she was already walking away.

I decided not to call her again until I had done it three times in a row. After another week I had really learnt how to hold the ball tightly with my fingers but with my hand relaxed then as the ball burst free it spun and almost whirred through the air.

One morning I woke up laughing from a dream. I had done it! And Monika was celebrating with me, joyfully dancing and tossing me around.

As I was practising later she came up and asked me, *Can you do it now?*

I think so, I replied not very confidently.

Show me.

I picked up the ball, paused for a moment, caught sight of the Magician in my mind's eye – and threw. I heard the whirr as the ball left my grip, it swerved around the pole and back into the tree trunk. I let out a cry of joy, jumped twisting in the air to face her as I came down. I was half expecting her to clasp me in her arms and toss me high into the air in delight. Instead she gave me a polite nod, went over to the stake, pulled it out of the ground and moved it a little to the left of the direct line.

Now bend it around from the left.

Before I could answer, she was striding away.

Bending the ball around from the left proved a lot harder for a right-handed person like me. A couple of weeks of futile practising went on before Monika came and stood for a long while watching me in a grey woollen sweater. When she finally spoke, I had forgotten she was there so her voice startled me.

I think you need help, come.

We walked over to the hall where she danced. This was built with five slightly unequal sized walls. Even without any heating a warmth met us as we entered. Diffuse light came from glazed windows set in the roof. There was a scent of wax, resin and oil from the wooden walls and floor. She left me in the middle of the hall and went to a cupboard built into a wall. I gazed up at the roof where delicate blue interwove with mauve and magenta. A moment later she was on her way back to me. My mouth dropped. She was carrying two mops.

She began demonstrating the art of mopping. I tried to follow her movements but my heart wasn't in it. I was hardly listening to her explanations, my eyes filled with tears. After a minute she took the mop from me and gave me a steely glance, *I can see you are not listening. Very well, if you will not learn the easy way, you must go down the rough track.*

We went outside. She made a throwing motion, three times she showed me the long even movements similar to casting a spear. A heavy shower began to fall as she left me to my practice.

That evening we ate in her home. She had made vegetable soup which we ate with unleavened bread from the village kitchen. I was sulky but the food tasted delicious.

Can we have a desert?

Not before we have had a talk. She motioned to the picture of the Magician on her otherwise bare wall. *For all the time you are in a state of grace* – she clicked her tongue, *I am forgetting, you are only few in years, for all those times when your throwing is filled with song, there are hours, days, weeks, months of practice. Learn the Magician's warning: Hard work alone will help you cross the bridge. Otherwise you will remain a poor player of tricks, with your mind not even set on what you are trying to do. That too was written by Empty Mountain*. She gave me a penetrating look, *Hard work, hard work and more hard work*.

I glanced up toward the picture but my eyes latched on two big tree-syrup and ground nut sweets on a shelf, the sweets were made in the shape of gnomes, *Monika?*

Her eyes followed mine, something like a twinkle came to them but her lips remained pursed. She shook her head, *Ah, but you are still a child. And perhaps the fault is mine that you think mopping is a punishment and the mop only a flunky copy of a lance*.

After we had eaten the desert and drunk herb tea sweetened with fruit cordial she spoke again, *You need to know that throwing is not done with the hands but with the heart*.

I looked at her perplexed.

She grunted, *Just as the blood flows all around the body after after its passage through the heart so all of you is engaged in the throw not just the hands. Learn to sense that you move with your whole body. Learn to feel what your toes, heels, the arches of your feet are doing when you throw. Grasp how the soles of your feet grip the ground. This you can do quicker with the mop–* she stopped, *But you are stubborn, something of the stiff-necked still lives in you.* She shook her head, rose and glanced out of the window, *Those who know about clouds might say, it will probably drizzle for days. But that is no reason to stop you practising.*

Next morning in a dream just before waking, I was watching Monika painting a huge picture of the First Arcanum. Without turning to me she said, *Practise, practise, practise.*

And somehow, with the Magician as my companion it became easier to practise hour after hour. Three more days and I had learnt to swerve the ball around from the left.

23. Weaving

Midsummer had passed, darkness began to cover the midnight sky. For some reason Monika didn't set me a new task, she kept me alternating between curving the ball around from the right and then from the left. I had got the hang of it and began to feel I needed something new. When I asked her if we could start a new task, she pondered for some time before drawing a circle large enough for me to stand and throw in about fifteen steps from a birch tree. Then she placed two staves in the ground between the circle and the tree, not quite in a straight line. The stave nearest to me was about half a pace to the right and the one further away about half a pace to the left of the direct line between the centre of the circle and the tree. She put her hand on my shoulder and gave me a keen glance before she explained this new play-practice, *Throw the ball to the right of the first pole, make it swerve around to the left of the second pole then make it swerve back to hit the trunk of the tree.*

I looked up at her in disbelief. Then I ran around to the right of the first stave on the right, curved round to the left of the second stave on the left and ran back to put my hand on the trunk of the birch. *Is that what you want?*

Yes, make the ball swerve in an 'S-form'.

What's an 'S'?

I still didn't know letters.

She made an irritated clicking sound with her tongue, *It's a letter shaped like this*, and she drew the form in the air.

I was baffled. The earlier spin and swerve throws were tricky enough, real tough for a seven year old, but at least I had the sense that they could be done, and so if I practised enough and refined my technique, I would eventually get the hang of them. But this new task: To spin the ball making it curve one way and then to get it to curve back on itself … this meant I'd have to make the direction change in flight, I'd have to change the spin after letting go of the ball and that was impossible, wasn't it?

Earlier I just practised. Sometimes I kicked the dirt in disgust, sometimes I tossed the ball jubilantly into the air to mark a success. But now I started to think about what I was trying to do. I realised that if I spun the ball, it would curve in a certain way and if I spun it the opposite way, it would swerve the other way. But once I'd let go of the ball – that was it!

The thought grew in me that the task was impossible and this stopped me from practising meaningfully. I began to imagine the staves as hooded assailants. One time I threw the ball and it glanced off the first pole and hit the second. I pictured the stakes as headless serpents writhing in front of me.

She noticed something had gone amiss with my practising and began to spend time observing my throws. This stopped me from playing at beheading serpents. She became even more taciturn as though she were reverting again to her maiden-aunt mode. I began to feel lonely and thought about Maria even more than usual. The Grey had not visited us since shortly before my birthday.

Perhaps because I had let the feeling grow in me that this play-practice was not possible, I started to resent her a bit. I wondered if she might have given me this task just to make fun of me. The thought came to me that I'd never really seen her throw so maybe she was trying to teach me something, she couldn't even do herself.

After about four more days of practising the 'S-swerve' I saw her coming to watch me – yet again. *Look, Monika*, I shouted as I threw the ball straight between the two staves and into the tree trunk, *What do you think of that?*

Throw it to the right of the first pole and bend it back from around the left of the second one.

I cast a ball to the right of the first stake, it flew in a direct line and didn't deviate at all.

Keep practising, Kell, she said in a flat voice.

I turned to see her walking away. *No Monika, look at this*. I threw a third ball, it glanced off the inside of the first stave, touched the second just enough to change its flight so it hit the tree trunk. I punched my fist in the air in triumph, *That's it, that's what you want isn't it?*

She strode over to me and seemed to grow in size or perhaps something in me shrank. Without a word she took the remaining balls from me. I had a sinking sensation I'd be sent to fetch mops. But she walked back and made another circle further from the tree than mine. She plucked up the two stakes and took a third.

Standing with her in the new circle I could see where she had set three poles. The first and third about a pace to the right and the second a pace to the left of the direct line from this circle to the tree trunk; they were evenly spaced. She guided me a few steps back and a little to the side so I was able to see clearly. Standing in the circle she tossed a leathern ball a couple of times in the air as though to get a feel for it then she became very still. All at once with a quick and purposeful motion she cast the ball. As before her movement was reminiscent to a javelin thrower's. I heard the characteristic whirr as it made a loop around to the right of the first pole and back toward the next. Suddenly the whirring note changed, the ball was swerving back toward the third, again the tone of the whirring altered as the ball veered around the right of the last stave and back to thump into the silvery trunk of the birch.

My mouth sagged. I glanced at Monika, she had

retained the posture of her follow through. Slowly she relaxed and turned to me, little emotion was visible on her face. I'd have been doing cartwheels, jumping up and down, cheering my success, clucking, strutting around and calling myself the cock of the hamlet if I'd done that.

She spoke softly, *It is called ball-weaving. The transition between getting a ball to swerve and to weave is one of the most difficult. Throwing is no longer my trade, Kell. Get one of the leaders of the Rangemen to show you what they can do.*

We stood looking at each other for a few moments without speaking.

Do they use calling stones?

How do you know that? she said sharply.

I, well er, Raynor gave me one.

What, Raynor! Her face hardened dramatically, *Show me!* She grabbed my upper arm so tightly that I let out a cry of pain. I was unceremoniously marched away.

Inside my room I pulled out the black stone from the back of the drawer and tentatively held it out to her. Her features softened, she took hold of the stone and caressed it with her fingertips. A misty expression stole into her eyes. *It is not finished, good! You may keep it.*

She insisted on us eating alone together that evening. I fell into silence, ashamed I'd thought she couldn't throw. Only as we were nibbling tree-syrup sweets moulded into the shape of birds like robins, did I venture to ask the question that was still bothering me, *Monika, once I've thrown a ball and its spin makes it swerve, how can I make it change its spin when I'm no longer touching it?*

Yes, that is the point. The ball will move under its own inertia as long as you are not connected with it. Inertia, yes, scientists in the seventeenth century coined that term, and it was a dominant theme in mechanics until the middle of the twenty-first century when events themselves proved their notions to be but metaphysical dogma – dogma with severe limitations!

I wasn't following at all. She put an arm around me, *You are quite right, Kell, only by remaining connected with the ball, can you make it change its spin.*

But I've let go of it!

Part of you remains with it.

Is it something to do with the ethric?

The etheric, mm, in a roundabout way.

You mean my etheric takes hold of the ball and changes its spin?

She started laughing, actually laughing. *No, no, Kell, to think that is to open yourself to inflation. And inflation can bring possession in its train.*

Eh?

Since you seem to have grasped the philosophical problem in a nutshell, I think you deserve a real explanation, in so far as I am able to give you one.

She seemed to fall into deep thought before shaking her head and standing up to make more herb tea. All at once she turned to me, a certain fire in her eyes, *Do you know the difference between a human being and an animal?*

Er?

If you think of sheep grazing, bleating or being herded together, if you look into their eyes, you will not find an individual looking back at you. If on the other hand you see a human being, you see a person. The person might be good, bad, weak, indifferent or angry but there is a real person there. Take Dungbjorn, he is one of a kind, there are no other Dungbjorns, there cannot be another Dungbjorn.

That's good, isn't it, Monika, only one Dungbjorn in the world.

She frowned, *Mm yes, very good, he is a unique individual.*

What has this got to do with spinning balls?

Oh, please be patient, Kell, existence is not so simple! The point is, this world came into being so that we could learn to become real individuals who can choose to do good or not to do good. We can choose to follow our ideals and aspirations, or we can indulge in our own greedy instincts. And we have become real persons. In much earlier ages of the earth our own unique individualities slept, as they say, in the wombs of the angelic hierarchies.

Eh?

We were sleeping, dreaming, we had not fully come down to earth. And to be aware of our own unique self, we had to become enclosed in our own skin. If a person thinks their body is their self, at least they realise they are a self. Going through Materialism and thinking of ourselves as separate bodies, was a kind of prerequisite for becoming aware of ourselves on earth as independent entities – and this brings it about that when we return to our true home in the heavens, we recognise ourselves as uniquely independent beings there too. Are you following, Kell?

Er, I thought we were talking about balls?

Yes precisely, monads! Her face was shining, *The human being is a unique monad or self separate from all other selves and able to make free choices.*

Monika, are there any more deserts?

She opened a cupboard and took out a ground nut and tree syrup sweet shaped like a flower, and put it absent mindedly into my outstretched hand. Her eyes seemed to be seeing beyond the four walls of her hut. Mine were fixed on the desert, I popped it whole into my mouth and chewed it lovingly.

Monika's voice seemed to be coming from far away, *In earlier ages, as Stoner made very plain for us, in Lemuria, human beings were not really down on earth, they did not know themselves as separate selves. Their astral and etheric bodies drifted over their physical forms. And these subtle bodies took hold of nature forces, not directly you understand, but their dreamy desires guided elementals – and darker human urges brought about great devastation in nature. Gradually though over the ages the etheric body of man drew ever closer to the physical one. The etheric brain eventually united with the physical brain – and the human being saw himself as an independent being. But because of the Fall of Man, he is ever tempted to think of himself as a body, as being nothing but a body.*

She paused. I thought I could taste flower essences in the sweet, lavender and mint, licorice and rose. And started to wonder what the etheric of flowers looked like.

She placed two cups of steaming herb tea on the table and sat down as she began speaking again, *The human etheric body joined together with the physical and thereby withdrew from the realm of the nature beings. People looked outside of themselves and perceived only surfaces. We saw only a nature bereft of her spirits. Her sprites, udines, gnomes and sylphs were thought of as being something in old wives' tales, as something non-existent. Mankind began to believe the forces of nature were independent of human thought and deed. Many even went as far as to believe that the so-called laws of nature could explain the coming into being of Man himself.*

Monika, can I had another desert?

She reached across and passed me a desert in the form of a little snail. I started to nibble its feelers.

Are you following, Kell?

We withdrew our feelers inside our skins?

Exactly! Very good. We looked out at the world and thought it was separate from us. But this is not really so, we are ever flowing outside ourselves, we stream outside our skins into our surroundings. Take the Greeks, they believed, no indeed they were aware of tactile arms shooting from their eyes.

Eh?

They realised that when they looked at something part of their own ethereal forces flowed out and touched what they were observing. It's the same with hearing. If your ears are blocked up not only do you not hear but you feel yourself cut off from your surroundings.

Can I have another desert?

She reached over and gave me a sweet shaped like a cat as she continued to speak, *When you follow the ball with your sight, you remain in delicate ethereal connection with it. This connection is very, very weak, your own ethereal forces can in no way take hold of the world outside you. But these etheric forces can guide elemental beings which are indeed able to effect changes in outer nature.*

She gave me a keen glance, *I did not change the spin of the ball, elementals followed my guiding sight and brought about the actual alteration of the spin and swerve.*

I had reached the cat's tail and wanted to make it last as long as possible.

Are you following, Kell?

Er, I follow the ball with my etheric eyes and get the elementals to do the hard work.

Well, you guide them by means of your etheric sight. The question is though whether the nature spirits will heed you or not. We cannot command them as did the magicians of yore. Shakespeare knew this.

She quoted a speech from one of his plays, there was something about a man breaking his staff and drowning his book. I now realise it must have been Prospero's speech:

"I'll break my staff, / Bury it certain fathoms in the earth, / And deeper than did ever plummet sound / I'll drown my book."

She concluded by saying, *So the elemental beings were to be free and no longer to be forced. The former magician himself was no longer able to command them, he was obliged to beg for their aid.*

She put her arm around me and hugged me to her, *You have done well, better than I expected. Back in my youth I read a book called "Zen in the Art of Archery", about how a philosopher took months, or was it years, to learn how to loose an arrow from a bow. What you have learnt to do is not dissimilar.* She ruffled my hair and went silent as I nibbled the last bit of the cat's tail. Then she added, *I never expected you to be able to ball-weave.*

Mm, these deserts are delicious.

She stood up and gave me another one shaped like a bull. I bit right into its horns as she went on, *If Maria were here, she probably wouldn't be able to hit the trunk of a birch from four paces but she might very well be able to ball-weave. With her conscious ethereal sight and her imagination she might have been able to guide a certain class of elemental beings which are quite capable of bringing about such physio-mechanical changes. I would never have allowed her to try though. It would be much too dangerous for her if she were able to do it. As it would be for you, if you got nature spirits to obey your whims.*

She looked at me fondly as she spoke, *But I thought since you had done the earlier exercises so well, I would just try ... and see what happened.* She turned her gaze to the picture of the Magician.

My teeth had gotten into the bull's eye but my belly was rebelling. I sort of groaned, *Is it okay if I leave the rest of the bull till tomorrow?*

Empty Mountain put it so simply, she said, *The White Magic of the future will come about when elemental beings regain their trust in man.*

I think I am going to throw up.

I lurched up and stumbled toward the door but didn't quite make it.

She made me change my clothes and put me into her own bed. She was taking my pulse, her other hand was on my brow, *How many nut sweets did you eat?*

Three or four or–

Then I think it's nothing worse than overeating. She shook her head, *How could I have given you so many sweets?*

A single candle standing on the table lit the room. I was sleepy. She was sitting on the bed beside me as she spoke, *Tomorrow we will have a break from play-practice. No throwing for you and, alas, no dancing for me. Shall we go for a walk?*

The sleepiness left me, *A walk, you mean outside, outside the village?*

Yes.

I goggled at her. I'd never been outside, well not lawfully outside, without the Grey One taking me. *Do you mean it, but isn't that, er, dangerous?*

Something like the beginning of a smile stole across her face, *Sleep my boy, tomorrow will bring what it will.*

24. Going Outside

Early morning, still a hint of redness in the Eastern sky. We were about to leave the hamlet. Monika wore a long brown woollen coat. I bounded away toward the rosy arch.

Where are you running off to young man?

To the archway.

She shook her head and held her hand out to me, I ran back and clasped it. She squeezed mine tightly for a moment. *There is more than one way to leave the village*.

We walked hand in hand down a gentle slope through an orchard where apple and pear trees grew, and drew near a line of shrubs behind which were taller trees. The path threaded through the berry-bearing bushes. A hushed atmosphere met us, I knew we were approaching the boundary of the village. Directly in front of us stood an opening broad enough for us to pass though side by side and as high as a tall man. It was made from two intertwining oaks whose trunks were no thicker than I could get my seven year old arms right round but ivy twisted around them and this was especially thick at the top of the archway.

Half a dozen paces for the opening something caused me to stop. She gave my hand a little tug but my feet remained planted to the ground. I looked up at her, trying to recall something. She was frowning down at me.

Monika, shouldn't we, shouldn't I, er, go by myself?

She put her hand to her mouth looking aghast, *Oh Kell, you are right, I am forgetting. It has been so long since I walked with someone into–* She gestured with her hand toward the archway, pausing as though in an attempt to find the right expression, *Yes of course, we must each go alone.* She let go of my hand, *Wait here.* And went through the opening. Ten strides further on from the archway she swivelled round and called to me with a lilt of song in her voice, *Now you.*

I knew what to expect, or thought I did, but as I passed under the ivy no rotting stench, no hissing sensation of fear confronted me. There was a sudden change of smell and atmosphere but it was more like a sleepy sweetness, a treacherous, drowsy, cloying sweetness. I yawned and felt like rolling up and burying myself under the folds of her long coat.

She opened her arms as though to take me into her embrace but brought them to a stop a few inches from me, held them steady for a moment then made a sudden cutting movement with her elbows. I heard a cracking sound a few paces away. Before I could think what this might be, something cold like wind and water seemed to splash in my face, Monika was blowing through pursed lips into my eyes. *If you let yourself fall asleep here, your dreams will soon be filled with nightmare.* She took my hand and we marched on quickly. I had the impression of walking in a dream and gradually waking. After a hundred paces the vegetation thinned, bushes were few, under my feet grew the grass which is found on mountain slopes. Nearly half a mile away lay the dark coniferous forest. A light breeze swirled around us. I wanted to run and skip but it felt good to be holding her hand.

We stopped a couple of hundred yards from the edge of the trees. *We will go no further, there is danger there that I will not expose you to.* Her eyes were intently searching the eves. She relaxed and gave me a friendly look, *Few indeed walk there. Even the Rangemen only enter in groups. One of our tasks in the village is to hold the trees at bay.* She moved her arm in a wide arc, *Look.*

I followed her movement, remembering how the woods had appeared from the distance on my first journey outside with the Grey One. Close to, the forest felt like an angry ocean waiting to surge up and engulf us.

Its growth is frightening. Trees spliced with cancerous genes from animals – but you are too young to know of those crimes. We work hard to hold off its roots. She pointed around, I could see charred roots and stumps of trees. *We can stop it but,* she paused looking out over the tops of the trees, *But in doing so we make ourselves conspicuous. I sense they know we have an outpost near here. Who knows when they may attack us.*

I must have looked shocked.

Don't worry, little one, we have our escape routes well prepared. They cannot take us all at once. Indeed they cannot move against us without a large force. And armies take time to prepare. The Rangemen would know of it. Not unless they sent one of the– she stopped and glanced down at me, touching my hair, lowering her face close to mine and speaking in a whisper, *But then I think the Grey would know of it and we would receive protection.* She turned again to the dark and ominous trees, raised herself to her full height and set her jaw, *Let them come!* She laughed. Free and loud her laughter sounded between us and the wood, *Yes, let them come, they will pay dearly. Maybe I will make this place my last stand.* She shook her fist at the forest.

Her action reminded me of something. In my mind's eye I saw the fist of Kaspar's drunken keeper and began to wonder if those, who planned that crime, were also responsible for bringing these spliced trees into the world.

She had taken my hand again and was pulling me gently away from the wood.

Can he go in there, can the Grey One enter this forest?

Where can he not go? But the Grey never takes risks unless the need is real.

We strolled slowly and thoughtfully back toward the village. Halfway back we caught sight of a hawk in the sky above us.

Did they hear my laughter? She spoke as if to herself, let go of my hand and made a wide circling movement with her arm which gradually spiralled in. The hawk flew down in loops and landed a few paces from us. She scrutinised the bird before speaking, *It is hard for the hunters, for the eagle, the falcon, the lion and the cat.* She fished something out of her pocket and tossed it toward the bird. It sprang up and in flight took the food in its beak. Monika waved her arm and the hawk rose into the sky. We followed its flight over the forest.

She made as it to walk back but stayed her motion and pointed a little to my right. I looked down and saw a tiny field mouse peeping through blades of grass. She glided toward it, holding a few crumbs in her outstretched palm. The mouse sniffed the air before coming cautiously closer to nibble from her hand. It hopped up onto her palm. She rose up holding the mouse gently but firmly and showed him to me. *Many are the creatures which suffer because of–* She motioned to the trees.

With one finger I stroked its smooth furry coat. Then she knelt down and stretched out her hand near the level of the ground. The mouse darted away, stopped, turned around and raised itself on its hind legs as though in a gesture of farewell before disappearing into the grass.

25. Flower Power

The sky was blue, the morning sun shining, there was little wind. I was practising cartwheels on a patch of grass in front of our home. Monika hadn't let me eat breakfast. I was very hungry. She called to me just as I managed to do a forward spring landing on my feet. She appeared in a pale blue dress and stood against the closed door of her dwelling holding out a little black bag. *What do you think is in this? No! No touching or sniffing. Can you make your mouth water?*

That was no problem at all, I was hungry. She held out the open bag toward me, though her hand was nearly closed around its neck so I couldn't see what it contained.

Spit into the bag.

What!?

Spit into it, she repeated firmly.

I did as I was told.

What can you taste?

I had the unmistakable taste of salt on my tongue. *Salt.*

She twisted back the neck of the bag and showed me the small amount of grey sea salt inside it. Then she retreated inside her home and closed the door behind her. I went back to cartwheels. A minute or so later she came out again holding another similar bag, *Spit into this.*

This time I detected a sweetness on my mouth.

What can you taste?

Er, something sweet, sugar?

She peeled back the neck of the bag to reveal light brown tree-syrup sugar. I reached out to take some in my fingers but quick as a cat she was gone with the bag closing the door behind her. She came out with a brown leather bag and repeated the procedure. When I spat, I couldn't get a taste at first but then it seemed like, *Bread?*

She showed me the little piece of dark brown bread contained in the bag.

A shaft of sunlight shone through her window and illuminated the table where we ate a late breakfast in silence. There were never deserts at lunchtime but as a treat I had been given half a teaspoonful of tree-syrup sugar.

Practice makes perfect so they say and it is true but only if you practise aright. One of the secrets of ball-weaving is to remain connected with the ball after you have let it go. This morning you have proved you remain connected with you saliva, your spittle, for a short while even after it has left your mouth when you are no longer physically connected to it.

Do I have to taste the ball?

She made a clicking sound with her tongue, *You use your tactile arms! The Ancient Greeks, as I told you, knew we aren't contained in our skin. They lived outside in the sunshine and the open air, they knew that from their eyes ethereal organs streamed out to touch what they were seeing.*

I pictured half-naked men and women by a sunny riverbank touching each other with long thin arms protruding from their eyes. One of the men was tickling a girl with his tactile arms. It looked so funny I started to giggle.

Her voice rose, *Not only through our eyes, through all our senses we go out into the world around us. As I told you, when your ears are blocked up you feel cut off. This is because you are unable to easily stream out etherically into your surroundings through your ears.*

I wasn't really following I couldn't remember my ears ever being blocked up. *Can cats go out through their ears?*

She frowned but nodded.

Last Summer an English family had told me a story about a Cheshire cat which could disappear leaving only its smile. I pictured a cat going out of itself, being sort of turned inside out, going out of itself through its own ears, leaving only two pointed cat ears sticking up in the air. It was so funny I burst out laughing at those imaginary cat ears left in mid air.

Monika could move with lightening speed. On a number of occasions I had seen her grab a fly in her hand. I believe she could have taken hold of a striking snake as easily as someone could intercept the movement of a sloth. She suddenly pounced on me, carrying me with two swift strides to the open window and pushing my nose between the bars. *Look outside, breathe the air, catch the fragrance of living plants.*

A moment later she had dumped me on a rug on the floor.

Here you are cut off from nature, caught up inside four walls, cooped up in yourself. When I speak about remaining connected, it is an ethereal connection; the very same as when you play outside in nature, when your senses linger in the sky and in the scent of flowers, and you are no longer just closed up inside the surface of your skin.

I sat in a heap on the rug looking up at her with an open mouth.

Children! Sometimes I think they can only come out of themselves through their mouths!

Dreamily I saw myself turning inside out of myself and jumping through my own wide open mouth; leaving only my lips stretching in the air and then with an elastic twang they snapped back to my mouth.

She was already continuing her discourse. *Stupid Moderns and Post-moderns from the twentieth and twenty-first centuries, they thought of themselves as being inside themselves. They thought they could only go out of themselves in their copul–* She stopped, her cheeks seemed to redden slightly, she turned away and tried to busy herself making more tea but wasn't able to stop her speech, *They, they looked out at life and thought their eyes were mini-cameras. They went out of themselves no further than taking snapshots. Click, click, click.* She held her hand up to her face and turned head as she said, *Click, click*. She was imitating someone taking a picture with a camera. Only at that time I didn't know what cameras were.

They took still-life pictures. They killed movement, snap, snap, snap. And then, do you know what they did?

I shook my head

After they had killed life's movement and made it into cold and changeless images, they warmed it up again. She laughed grotesquely. *They warmed it up, they ran the still pictures one after another: zip, zip, zip, zip, zip*. She made a movement with her right hand as though turning a wheel. *The films they made, you know what they called them?*

I shook my head. I didn't know anything about cameras and had never seen a film.

They called them art. Art! Can you imagine that?

I was on the point of asking what art was, but thought better of it. She was speaking rapidly her Russian accent becoming more pronounced, her movements had a wildness to them I had never seen before.

It was the same with their science. Differential equations, bah! She spat and rubbed the spit in the rug with her socking foot. *To get the derivative they stopped time, they killed movement. Imagine that! Bigwig physicists trying to stop time! And do you know what they did next?*

I wasn't following at all.

They tried to warm up their frozen life pictures, they tried to solve differential equations by integrating– and as if rounding off her case for the prosecution she added, *Numerically!* She was looking straight ahead with an almost smug expression on her face. *Kantians all of them, never believing they could know the thing-in-itself, never seeking to learn to live outside themselves in nature's ceaseless life.* She looked straight at me, *Do you believe you can know the thing-in-itself, Kell?*

Monika can I have a tree-syrup sweet, one made like a badger? They were the biggest.

She'd quietened down but didn't seem to have heard my question. *Kant loved Newtonian dynamics with its concept of changeless inertia.*

What's Newtopian Dominoiacs?

Listen, Kell, if you throw a ball it will just go straight, if you throw it with spin it will curve one way and that's it. To guide a change in motion you have to remain connected, but you aren't physically-mechanically connected of course. Do you understand?

I dropped my head. She growled in irritation and went to the cupboard. She came back with a badger, a nut-syrup sweet shaped like a badger. I went to sit at the table and nibbled its nose. She sat beside me looking way off into the distance or perhaps deep into her own thoughts.

Monika, I like it when you talk filosopsy. I think I said it because of the badger. I'd have happily listened to her canting on about Newtop if it meant I could get my teeth into a tree-syrup sweet.

She turned to me with narrowed eyes almost as though reading my thoughts, *Philosophy! Philosophy, Kell*,

I quickly bit off the butt of the badger in case she

recanted and took the sweet away from me.

Don't you see it's the same. It doesn't matter whether a physicist freezes motion in a differential equation or a photographer takes still pictures that they then try to put back together; one still life after another to make a lifeless copy of outer action. Kill movement in a frame then put the frames back together to make a semblance. Don't you see it's the same paradigm?

I bit off the badger's head.

She sighed, *The Humpty-Dumpty syndrome*.

I'd heard of him, from inside me I repeated the rhyme in English:

Humpty Dumpty sat on a wall
Humpty Dumpty had a great fall
All the king's horses and all the king's men
Couldn't put Humpty together again.

Precisely, Kell! Rip it apart, take the life out of it and then try to fix the dead bits back together. Scientists right up to nearly the middle of the twenty-first century thought they could pull apart and put back together again – all without any consequences. She leaned toward me, dark tones in her voice, *Make life out of little bits of dead things*.

I shuddered.

Let me teach you a bit of history. You do know what history is don't you?

I looked the other way and nibbled the badger's belly.

They got rid of pictures and instead made dots. Tiny dots of coloured light, millions of dots on screens. And billions of people, billions of children hunched up over the screens, pressing buttons or pushing the mouse.

Monika?

Yes?

Didn't the mice run away when they let go of them?

She crinkled her brows but went on undeterred, *It got worse, far, far worse. They started chopping up bits of DNA, splicing genes. Crossing jelly fish with guinea pigs*.

I pictured a guinea pig with long slimy tentacles coming out of its back end.

And salmon the size of sharks. Salmon biting the butts of grizzly bears. She sighed, *And then they started to remake creatures long extinct*.

I felt sad. I was down to the badger's front paws and started to wonder if those jean splizer's could remake the sweet from just its paw.

They thought they could cut up bits of living things and put the lifeless bits back together but jumbled up. Humpty Dumpty all over again. No wonder Humpty Dumpty was always drawn as an egghead in children's books of rhyme. She curled her finger to bid me to come closer, *The scientists did not realise (what their Falarch masters had long planned) that when their spicings were pitched out into the wilds, they multiplied ... and thus the world changed*. A look of bitter satisfaction appeared on her face as though she had let me in on tragic world secrets.

I was wondering if I dared ask for another badger.

Monika?

Yes?

The moment I spoke, I knew it wasn't on to beg for another badger so I found myself asking her another question, *Can you tell me more about being ethelly connected?*

Ethereally, ethereally connected. She grunted and got up from the table and busied herself again with the tea pot.

I felt very tired, lay down on the rug, stretched out and was soon sound asleep.

In my dream I was throwing leathern balls at a thin stave. On my left Miss and Moppar were watching, eager to go after the balls I was throwing. On the other side sat Djorki, he too seemed to want to chase the balls. Then I saw lights around the dog yet as I looked at them they disappeared. I turned to the cats, there were lights about them too. I tried to see the lights without really looking at them. Gradually the lights became shimmering figures which had something like wings. I realised they too concentrated on what I was doing. Only whereas the cats and the dog were looking at the balls, the diffuse figures were only interested in my movements. I spoke to them, *Can you help me move the balls in the air?*

The figures seemed to merge and become smaller. Then one separated out from the others and came toward me, he gazed up and nodded in affirmation.

Then make it bend to the right.

He shook his head.

Why not?

The fairy figure coalesced again with the others. He emerged to answer with a clear childlike voice, *We can't see the ball properly, we see your connection to it. You have to remain connected.*

I felt anger inside me, I wanted to cast a ball at him. Somehow I managed to hold back the anger and threw the ball at the stave instead. I noticed how strings of ethereal light were attached to the ball from my fingertips and from my eyes. The elemental figures flew up and followed the ball dancing around in the air and laughing. The ball itself seemed to be moving in slow motion. Out of the corner of my eye I noticed Moppar growing to huge size, he leapt up and knocked me to the ground, his jaws clutched my hand. I could feel his teeth entering my flesh, I yelled–

And opened my eyes, the dream had gone, the cat was trying to nip my fingers as they twitched in sleep.

Monika was looking down at me, *You must have been*

very busy in your dream.

I stumbled to my feet, *Can you tell me more about being ethrelly connecting?*

Ethereal, being ethereally connected.

She guided me to the table and sat me in a chair, took a flowering plant in a pot from the window sill and put it in front of me, *Touch the flower.*

As I reached out to touch it, she drew the plant away.

Touch but don't touch. Open your hand and hold it an inch or so from the flower and ... let us see what happens.

After about half a minute I began to feel a warmth in the palm of my hand, warmth and movement, rounded movements. *Monika, I –*

She put her finger to my lips, *To the greenhouse!*

There were all sorts of flowers in the greenhouse. I wandered around opening my palm to them. What surprised me was how different the sensations I experienced were. Some flowers felt warm and had sleepy rounded movements, others were light with almost spiky in-and-out motions. After some minutes I began to feel really tired. Monika noticed and took me out of the greenhouse.

We were standing on the lawn in front of our home. The sun was still shining brightly.

Now you begin to realise what being ethereally connected means – your etheric meets the etheric of the flowers.

I stood looking at the grass, my gaze lifted to bushes and trees. I began to be aware of how plants were filled with living forces, invisible etheric life forces. And I remembered how last Summer I had promised myself that one day, one day I too would learn to see this ethereal world. I wasn't able to to yet but I was learning to touch it. And maybe my sight would open when I became more aware of tactile arms streaming from eyes.

A deep longing arose in me to see my sister, to be with her and to share the sight of the hidden elemental world that she knew so well.

I became aware that Monika was speaking … *the world was not only driven along by amoral science and technology powered by immoral financing. In the nineteen sixties a medicine was made directly from the etheric of flowering plants, 'Exaltation of Flowers' it was called. Via the sensitive human hand the etheric life force in a flower was drawn into and retained in spring water. Many flower powers were combined as the calm at the centre of a storm. It was even sold in health shops and written about in books like 'The Secret Life of Plants'.*

Monika? She had been gazing into the light-filled sky but squinted down at me as I spoke, *Can you remind me what a shop is?*

Ah Kell, have you not followed what I have been speaking about?

I bowed my head.

Her voice softened, *Perhaps later, perhaps much later you will remember what we have spoken about.* She gave me a hug and whispered, *I have a ground nut sweet shaped like a flower, would you like to –*

Eat it!

She nodded.

You bet! Race you to the door!

I bounded off. Ten yards from the door I glanced around, she was nowhere to be seen. I ran on without thinking, without really looking and ran straight into her outstretched arms. She folded them around me and twizzed me around in the air. She had been waiting by the door for me.

How, how did you–

She shook her head back and forth, *A lot, Kell, you've got such a lot to learn.*

26. Dung Spotting

Monika was much younger, her golden hair streaming out behind her as she ran and dived into a lake. She bobbed up from the water's surface, waved me to join her and began to sing. I ran toward her but tripped over a tree root. My body in the bed gave sudden lurch in sympathy. The song in the dream was that in my room but the dream pictures slipped away in a twinkling. I sat up and rubbed my eyes and saw her gazing down at me through the connecting space. Her song ended with quiet longing. I listened to the lingering stillness.

Your breakfast awaits you.

When I entered her home I glanced across at the flowering plant in the pot and lifted my hand almost as if to wave to it or perhaps to sense its etheric forces with my own.

She noticed, *Yes, Kell, when you have opened your palm to a plant, it is no longer a thing. There is more to it than meets the physical eye. You look but a questioning lingers in your looking and a longing arises within you to know what is active within that which you see.*

Funny how whenever she started talking about philosophy, I felt like eating something sweet. *Are you filosopsizing?*

Philosophising, Kell, philosophising.

What's in the jar? I pointed across at a ceramic jar on the table.

Honey.

What's that?

Ah child, bees were almost the first thing to go after the splicings infected the world. They looked like wasps.

Wasps! I had been fingering the honey pot but withdrew my hand as if I'd been stung when she said that.

Don't worry bees could sting, yes, but they didn't unless provoked. They ate only nectar from flowers mixing it with pollen and their own secretions to make honey. Would you like some?

Another time maybe, Monika.

It's sweet.

Oh!

Honey is very rare nowadays, we have few jars left. It is eaten at special times in memory of honey bees.

She smeared a thin layer of honey on dark bread and handed it to me. As the wholesome taste of the bread melted with the sweet tang of the honey in my mouth, the picture came to me of that little bottle from which the Grey One had once added a few drops to the bitter herb medicine I was given after my first venture outside the hamlet. *The Grey's medicine is it, er, is it anything to do with that exalting flowers, that flower power medicine you told me about yesterday?*

You are more perceptive than you appear. I must have looked blankly back at her because she repeated what she'd said in more understandable terms, *You aren't quite as dumb as you look. Yes, the Grey uses a similar technique but not only with plants also with minerals, metals and crystals. And drawing hidden ethereal forces from flowers is easy compared to crystals. For the etheric body of a plant is within but that of a crystal outside. As like as not mountains of play-practice with crystals lie before you.*

In the back of my mind I saw the unfinished black calling stone Raynor had given me and thought I would get him to show me how he uses the finished stones.

She broke into my thoughts, *I don't know if you are to be a thrower and captain of the Rangemen or–* she paused, *Or maybe a healer.*

A healer! But, Monika, I want to be a knight, a fighter.

Brat! Is your ambition to cause wounds rather than heal them? Outside and practise – now – this very minute.

She bungled me out of her home. There was a cry in my voice as I asked her what I should practise.

Cartwheels and, er– the hardness in her features dissolved into a wry smile, *And go and feel the glowing etheric of red and white roses*.

At lunchtime we ate in the hall with the others. Monika took only a small porting of vegetable pie. I had a little slice of roast lamb with my pie. She never or almost never ate meat. I ate mainly grains, salads and vegetables but occasionally took a slice of meat. A couple of times a week meat was on the menu. Monika let me eat what I wanted but she would frown if I put too much meat on my plate.

My sister had never tasted meat in her life. The first time meat was served after she arrived, she had a piece of lamb on her plate. She put it into her mouth and chewed on it a couple of times before spluttering, *What's this?*

Mutton – sheep meat, said Monika dryly.

Maria opened her dark eyes wide and stared at her in disbelief, she glanced at me and back at Monika – and spat. She spat everything in her mouth right out all over the table and rushed out of the hall crying. I was trying to rub a little piece of meat off my nose as the people around us began muttering and tutting. Monika's sharp look quailed them. After that Maria would not come into the hall if meat were on the menu.

As I stuck my fork into the lamb, a thought struck me. Monika and Maria didn't eat meat and they could see the etheric but we who ate meat couldn't. *Monika, if I stopped eating meat would I be able to see ethrelly?*

See the etheric, you mean. It's not as simple as that, Kell, just to stop eating meat would not give you the capacity for clear sight in the etheric. On the other hand eating too much meat might hinder you from seeing invisible life forces. Most people would do well to eat a little less meat.

I cut my slice of lamb into two pieces and resolved only to eat one of them. After I had eaten the rest of the meal, the little half slice still remained. I was sorely tempted to gobble it up. *Why is meat served? If we didn't have meat on the table we wouldn't be tempted to eat it, would we?*

True but– she glanced across at Dungbjorn who was gesticulating loudly on another table, *The Bjorns of this world would fall apart if they didn't eat some meat.*

Dungbjorn bit deeply into a lamb shank, fat from the meat dribbled down into his beard. Contrary to rules his dog was sitting under the table gnawing a bone. Dung looked across at us chewing with his mouth open and waved. Except for the guards he was about the only person in the hamlet not abashed by Monika. She nodded slightly in response. Then, to judge by the change in her expression, something must have struck her. *Come Kell, let us have a walk.*

We'd been walking all around the village and she hadn't let me speak. Finally she stopped and looked down at me just as I kicked a little stone, *Play-practice. You have done very well at throwing, much better than I had expected. And even if you had been able to ball-weave I would have had to stop you at once; you are far too young to be commanding elementals! You have learnt to touch plants etherically, you have as it were learnt to use your etheric hands. This practice can continue but it mustn't be overdone; it is too strenuous. But your etheric sight, mm, I want to give you a little exercise to prove to you the truth of tactile arms. She started to explain herself ...*

I felt like a newly recruited Rangeman as I crept around the hamlet. My task was to spy on Dungbjorn, to sneak up behind him and to fix my eyes on the back of his neck … and see what happened.

I caught sight of him, busying himself knocking together a rough piece of furniture. I sneaked behind a water barrel and stared at the back of his neck, willing my sight to bore into him. He'd been singing for some while or perhaps spluttering would have been a better description of the noise he was making. Twenty seconds or so after I fixed my eye on him he stood up straight, scratched the back of his neck and turned around. I dodged behind the barrel. When I peeped out a bit later he was back at his work. I focused on the back of his neck again. This time the effect took place after only about ten seconds. He turned around and stared about just as I pulled back behind the barrel. When I peered out again he was still gazing about so I waited until I could hear him hammering before trying to fix my stare on him again.

The whole thing was repeated about three or four more times. I was finding it harder and harder not to laugh at his stupid expression when he looked about. Then he called to his dog and mumbled something to it. Next time he got back to work, the dog was lying beside him on its front paws. I put my arrow-eye on the back of his neck once more. The moment he stopped his work, the dog began to bark. Dung was too slow to notice but not the dog. I had been spotted while Dungspotting.

I darted behind the barrel but could hear the dog bounding toward me, it appeared and started barking at me. Dung came into view. He grabbed me by the scruff of the neck and lifted me up holding onto my coat just behind my neck. *What we here have?*

I was dangling and kicking. A woman came out of a hut

and pointed at me, *The witch boy has been putting the evil eye on you, I've been watching him.* She came closer and looked as though she might scratch my eyes out as she lisped, *The naughty, wicked creature.*

Put me down, put me down! I was trying to punch his arm and kick him but my punches had no effect and his arm was too long for my kicks to reach him.

He was laughing, *He no witch boy, he Monika boy. And Dung thought sliced people were spying on him!* He smiled at me, one of his front teeth was broken. *No need Monika spy on Dung. If Monika want know Dung, she come to him. Plenty room between me and Mutty.*

I heard a loud bark, Djorki was racing toward us. Monka was in view and called him back. Dung put me down. The woman had gone back into her hut and closed the door by the time Monika came up.

Good afternoon, Mr Dungbjorn. I had Kell test you, test how sensitive you were. She looked across at me, *Well?*

Eh?

Was he sensitive?

I nodded.

Dungbjorn pushed himself up proudly and prodded his chest, *Dung super-sensitive!*

As we were walking away he added, *Dungbjorn like Monika.*

She didn't stop or turn but a kind of almost girlish smile appeared on her face for a moment. Maybe Monika really did have a soft spot for Dung.

Trespassing Kell, your tactile arm, your etheric sight was trespassing upon his etheric. This is definitely not something to practise but I wanted to prove to you that sight isn't passive. Light doesn't just shine into the retina of your eye, your own invisibly shining ethereal forces stream out from your eyes to touch – and trespass – upon that which you look upon. Once is enough! To practise such things belongs to the black path or at least to a grey one.

But Monika, isn't the Grey's path good?

She smiled broadly and once again I noticed a kind of girlish charm transforming her features, she was shaking her head as she spoke, *He let's us call him the Grey because of Gandalf. He read 'Lord of the Rings' as a boy and was enthralled by it. His is the white path but sometimes, as in the book itself, those who appear white are not what they seem, and some who look grey are in reality purest white.'To look foul and feel fair', or something like that. He even called the Rangemen, 'Rangemen', after Aragorn's Rangers.*

We were quiet for some while. I had still not entirely got over the shock of being caught spying. Djorki was lying on the hearth. I lay down beside him. Miss jumped down from the window sill and began to push up against me purring.

Remember, Kell, if people practise trespassing sight, they are on the wrong path.

That evening she was holding my hand after finishing a Norwegian fairytale about a troll. I was mischievously imagining myself chasing Dung all around the hamlet tickling him with my etheric sight, with shining rays of light streaming out from my eyes.

Stories about saints and fables are to come after the Summer and some geography as well but I don't know, Kell, what your next play-practice is to be. You have done enough throwing for this Summer. Cartwheels and touching plants ethereally you can keep doing but not too much. Mm, we could get you climbing trees – no, Autumn is at hand, dark is returning, I will not risk you falling and being injured. Troubles might coming even here to the hamlet. What is the best play-practice for you, I wonder?

I turned over and lay on my side and got back to pretending to tickle Dung with tactile arms.

27. Where Have All the Dancer's Gone

We had spent most of the evening quietly sitting outside Monika's home. A couple of gnats had buzzed around us which was very unusual. She'd mumbled something about the border being in need of repair. And I began to wonder why mosquitoes abounded outside the village but never or only very rarely entered. There was no physical barrier to deter them from flying over the hedges so there must be some secret force holding them back. If only I could find the right way to ask her. *Who will repair the border?*

She began tapping her finger impatiently.

I tried another approach, *Is there some ethic force holding the gnats back?*

She opened her ageless eyes wide and looked at me intently, *Ethereal force. Good, Kell, but not now. I have been pondering your lessons. Be quiet a little longer.*

I went into my imagination wondering what the etheric forces around the hamlet might look like. I pictured shining vibrant colours reaching skyward in contrast to the darker opaque colourings driving the swarms of mosquitoes outside the village.

Gradually I became aware of her humming a tune. She began to sing softly in English. I listened carefully to her words. *Where have all the dancers gone–*

You're singing in English.

Yes, but I have changed the words a little. The song is, well was, very well known. And the sentiment fits. More than two centuries ago Stoner said – or it is said that he said – that there were more than a hundred thousand dancers in England alone.

England?

Yes, it is time you learnt a little geography but not just now. Today I want to tell you about a quest I undertook many years ago when I first heard about Stoner's utterance. That those hundred thousand, or was it two hundred thousand, didn't become dancers is clear enough, they did not. So what did they do? And was there something special about England or did the same apply to all countries or at least to many European lands? If I had been a man I might have got the answer much quicker. As it was, I had to go a roundabout way via history. History, you know what that is, don't you? It's about what happened in earlier times. Outside there is a lot of space, a whole earth. And knowledge of the earth is called geography. But there is also a lot of time, time gone by and time still to come. And knowledge of times past is called history. In ancient days there were Mysteries – She leaned toward me and set her elbows on the little rickety table between us, cupping her chin in her hands, *Don't ask.*

She settled back in her chair. *There were Mysteries and there were, em, dancer-movers we might call them. Where did such students of movement go when Greece and Rome dwindled into the Middle Ages?*

My mouth was about to open but she was too quick, she had already put her forefinger to my lips as she spoke, *In the Middle Ages who were those who practised movement?* She was looking straight at me, *Well?*

I guess that particular question wasn't meant to be rhetorical.

Er, er?

I would have thought the answer would have been very easy for you. You always seem to be thinking about the – the ones who move.

Eh?

I could see her impatience growing, I was afraid she might just get up and leave.

Er, er, er?

She was tapping her fingers again.

Then, I don't know quite how, it came to me, *Knights, they were the knights.*

She nodded, *I thought I might have been going a bit too far too fast for you but since you seem to have grasped or guessed that, I think I can venture a little further. The knights bore the true lineage not only of the warrior but also of the dancer in the Middle Ages. Yet once the Renaissance came and that coward's weapon, the gun, made the sword, the lance and even the arrow obsolete – where then did the dancers go?*

She sang the verse again:

Where have all the dancers gone
Long time passing
Where have all the dancers gone
Long time ago,
Where have all the dancers gone
Gone to be sportsmen everyone.

I have always loved Pete Seeger's song, "Where Have All the Flowers Gone", I hope he will forgive me for changing a few of the words.

She stood up and took a step away from the table. *Sportsmen then, and sportswomen, though here we meet another tragedy. For whenever something good arises in the world, Falarchs always seek to undermine the quality of innocence.*

Her eyes narrowed, *Are you following, Kell?*

Sportsmen were the new knights.

Exactly!

She gave me a pat on the back almost as if I'd achieved something significant in play-practice. *Come, we will inspect the border together and I will begin to teach you other forms of play-practising.*

She was away in an instant, I had to run as fast as I

could to catch her up. Djorki gave a bark and ran after us. Monika turned sharply around and gazed at the dog which stopped and put its head on the ground between its front paws, whining softly. She smiled, well almost, *Maybe even you might be useful*. She was off but the dog remained where he was until she turned back and called him.

Kell, I want no interruptions. You can watch but not, not a single question, is that understood?

I nodded but if I had been a dog I might have put my head between my paws and whined.

We had gone around the perimeter about a couple of hundred paces when we came across Miss and Moppar jumping after flies. Behind them one or two of the bushes were wilting. She walked up to them and touched their withered leaves then pointed down to a little patch of freshly dug earth, *I wonder what has happened here? Djorki fetch me one of the guards*.

The dog let out a friendly bark and bounded away. The cats chased after him but gave up halfway back to the guards dwellings and started to chase each other instead. Meanwhile Monika began prodding the loose earth with a stick. She shoved it in deeply and lifted. The body of a half-chewed rat came up. The remains of its dirty brown fur resembled pigs bristles, its fangs were over proportioned, its stench overpowering. I was trying to retch when Djorki arrived back with a guard.

Kell, go and play with the cats, far from here, and take Djorki.

The dog leant against me and pushed me away, my stomach was still trying its best to vomit. A few steps further on came the relief of a fresh breeze. Marigolds were swaying to its motion. The skies were clear and illumined with that special Scandinavian light. Miss and

Moppar were purring loudly as they tried to weave in and out of Djorki's legs.

I pictured the body of the rat and knew it was a manipulated rodent. I was too young to put this into words but the feeling was all the more intense for the lack of verbal articulation: Nature with human help and empathy would bring forth peace and plenty as well as loveliness but we had been sidetracked into splicing and manipulating, we had poisoned her. And I felt the "we", not the they. Somehow I sensed we were all to blame even such as me who weren't even born when the manipulated organisms had been designed, spliced, bred in laboratories and cast forth onto the breast of Mother Earth. I wanted to embrace the whole of nature but could only throw my arms around Djorki's neck and hold him tightly.

The dog stood still and allowed me to hug him. Then he gave a low growl. I looked up to see Dungbjorn tramping toward us. He passed by, he was going to Monika who at the same time was coming toward us.

My Mutty bad, help Mutty. Dung's voice had an eerie wailing quality to it. Suddenly he cast himself onto his knees before her, *Help Mutty, please Mutty save!*

She retreated half a pace before quickly recovering and lifting him up under the arms. *Don't kneel to me. I will help if I can but I am no vet.*

I followed after them. Dungbjorn's dog was lying in front of his little hut whimpering. It held up a leg with a sore of blood and pus.

Dung held his dog's head as she took its paw and inspected the wound. She frowned and turned to the guard, *We know now what happened but whether the dog attacked the spliced rodent inside the village or outside and then brought it back in, that would be worth knowing.* She spoke to Dungbjorn who was kissing the head of his dog. *How did it get the wound?*

Me no know, me no see Mutty, then Mutty came back with– he pointed at the wounded leg. *Help Mutty, Monika help Mutty, no?* His face was red, his jaw trembling as he spoke to her in broken English.

Come to think of it, he also spoke broken Norwegian, even one of his front teeth was broken.

She was already standing up, commanding the guard to fetch hot water and moving to collect her medicines.

Dungborn held his dog's head, it whined and whimpered but put up little resistance as she washed the wound, put on a few drops of tincture, bandaged it, set a little ointment over the bandage then wound more bandage around it. Finally she got Dung to open its mouth so she could let a few drops of two different tinctures fall onto the dog's tongue.

She rose and walked away from the dog. Dungbjorn came to her, *Be Mutty well?*

The bite itself is not deep but this was a spliced rodent and they carry fowl diseases in their spit.

Dungbjorn hate splicers, me kick them hard between legs, they no have childs, they no make more manipulated spring offs. Dungbjorn kick them hard!

Dung made a vicious kicking motion. And I a pretty certain if a gene-manipulator had taken that between the legs, he would never have been able to father a child.

She put her hand on his huge forearm, *Dungbjorn, there is something you can do.*

Me do anything for Mutty.

You can pray.

Dungbjorn hold Mutty all night in his arms, Dungbjorn pray all through night.

We turned to the dog, Djorki was standing by it and licking its head.

Stars were beginning to shine in the deep blue above us.

As she sat on my bed holding my hand, I asked her if the dog would get well. She shook her head, *It is beyond my power to heal it*– she got up and peered out of the window, *But not beyond heaven's. We too can pray.*

How can I pray?

You can picture the angel of the dogs lifting Mutty to the heavens in supplication.

Just as I fell asleep, I imagined a mighty winged angel with star-bright eyes lifting the dog out of Dung's arms and holding it up toward the heavens.

28. Dribbling

In a dream I saw Kaspar stroking his horse and thought to myself that he loved his wooden horse as much as Dungbjorn loved Mutty. *Mutty*, I said aloud and woke in the same instant. I jumped out of bed and opened the door. Monika was standing on her own doorstep.

Get dressed, Kell, before we go to see what the night has brought to the morning.

Dungbjorn's door was open, he was fast asleep in a low chair, his mouth half open. He seemed to have been dribbling down his beard. The dog lay on his lap. It opened its eye and looked at us.

She was stroking its head when he woke with a grunting, slobbering sound and tried to focus his eyes, *Mu–* before he finished speaking the word he was hugging his dog.

Easy, easy. Let us first tend the wound.

When we eventually got back to her home, she told me to wait outside. After a couple of minutes she came out with a ball of sown leather. It was round and about as big as my head.

What's that?

A football – or as near to a football as I can make here. I was not able to sleep, I spent the night stitching it together.

She tossed the ball to me. She was wearing trousers and snugly fitting boots. She noticed me looking at her clothing.

Some things are best not done in dresses. Throw me the football.

She was already moving from the door as she spoke. I tossed it toward her, she danced two steps back and caught the ball on her outstretched right foot and remained perfectly still for a couple of seconds. With a slight movement of her leg she sent the ball into the air and caught it on her left foot. She was juggling with the football: right foot, left foot, right knee, left foot, right foot, then she sent the ball into the air and caught it on her head. She ran off with the ball balanced on her hairline. Many years later when I first saw a seal balancing a ball on its nose, I was reminded of her balancing the football on her forehead as she ran.

With a slight bend she sent the ball into the air and threw herself backwards and, in what I later learnt was a bicycle kick, she shot the ball back at me. I took it full in the face. As she kicked the ball she'd been laughing but she was on her feet and taking hold of me as I slumped toward the ground. My eyes were smarting but I was determined not to cry.

A good thing it wasn't a real football or you would have been sporting two black eyes in the morning. Let's begin play-practice, pass me the ball. No, not with your hands, your feet!

We began passing the ball to and fro, one touch. We moved around the compound passing to each other. Finally she told me to run with the ball at my feet: right foot, left foot, keeping the ball as close to me as I could. I tripped over a couple of times and went sprawling, luckily the ground was fairly soft. Sometimes the ball just ran away from me.

She seemed pleased and spoke English because, as she said, in England football found a home.

Now Kell, dribble me.

But Monika, I'm thirsty, I've got no spit.

She took the ball off my foot with her own. *Now tackle me, take the ball off me. Not with your hands, your feet!*

She let me take the ball off her a few times then she said, *Now I'm going to dribble you.*

I looked up half expecting her to spit at me. She moved forward with the ball toward my right. I moved to intercept her but she swayed to the left and was past me.

A body swerve, Kell. I will teach you not only football but its history. Stanley Matthews was a master of the body swerve. His feet were quick but as defenders were watching his feet he was swerving, dancing passed them. Now try to dribble me.

I moved with the ball to her left, she took it deftly off my toe.

Enough now. But you have done well, much better than with any other play-practice. I'm so glad I thought of teaching you sports.

She moved off juggling the ball from foot to foot much faster than I could run.

In Britain many, perhaps most of the major sports were given their form: Football, cricket, tennis, rugby, golf, even boxing.

I thought you said, they started in England?

She sighed, *Geography, we'll soon have to begin geography lessons*.

Just as we were about to go in, we heard a shout. Dungbjorn was running toward us though perhaps lumbering would have been a better description of his motion.

Monika! Mutty eating, Mutty eating!

He reached toward her, a look of surprise appeared on her face as he took her in his arms. I flinched half expecting one of his bones to break but she let herself be lifted and tossed into the air. He caught her with surprising gentleness and set her on her feet.

Monika big Medicine Man. No, Monika big Medicine

WO-man!

He bowed low and set his forehead on the ground at her feet. Instead of trying to lift him as before, she knelt beside him and put her own forehead on the earth as she said, *Dungbjorn big prayer-man. Dungbjorn's prayers saved Mutty.*

The surprise on his face transformed into a joyous grin as he shouted, *Dungbjorn's prayers, Monika's medicines.*

As he rose up she prodded him hard in the chest and said in a commanding voice, *Don't let your dog eat too much!*

29. Duncan, Jack and Victor

Monika was still wearing trousers and a bulky woollen sweater as she stood gazing into the afternoon sky, clouds were gathering.

I almost feel young again with a football in my hands. A playfulness seemed to have replaced her usual dour expression. *Let us kick a ball to each other without letting it touch the ground.*

She kicked the ball into the air, it dropped toward my feet, I kicked, the ball spun off at right angles.

Two, she said, *Pick it up and kick it back to me.*

I kicked it high, it was going over her head but she moved backwards, five rapid walking steps while still facing me, and caught the ball on her right foot, knocked it forward to her left, back to her right, juggling the ball as she returned to where she'd started and sent the ball to me. I kicked at it, the ball spun backwards behind me.

Three, she said, *An improvement.*

I couldn't work out if she were making fun. She gathered the ball and kicked it to me again. This time I connected properly. She headed the ball and, just before it reached the ground, she scooped it up with her foot and back to me. I kicked it, the ball spun sideways off my foot, she moved – I don't know whether to say leapt, bounded or walked or a kind of mixture of all three – and just managed to reach it with her toe before it landed.

Five, progress continues.

This was difficult play-practice. We must have spent more than an hour at it. She was very patient as long as she felt I was making a real effort. But her face became stern as that of a stone statue when I gave way to my frustration and kicked angrily at the ball. Her look was enough to chide me; I remembered Djorki with his paws between his legs whining.

Eventually we managed to get a total of seven in this back and forth passing before the ball landed. She seemed genuinely pleased. I too felt I was learning fast, most of all because of imitating the way she moved. I was hoping we would reach ten but she stopped suddenly.

You are copying my movements too closely, Kell. Here we stop. You are to practise ball juggling on your own for at least half an hour.

The most I got to was four. In anger I picked up the ball and slammed my foot into it, if I had connected properly it would have risen high into the air, it just slid off sideways.

Kell! She was framed by the door, *Pick up the ball and come in at once.*

I felt deflated to have been caught in this very act of petulance.

On her table were three pieces of paper. Paper was not easy to come by. She had made three charcoal drawings and covered them with a fixing liquid which was drying. Three men wearing funny clothes and boots (football kit, she said it was). Each man had a ball at their feet and they were in the very act of going past a defender. Monika described it as 'leaving the defender for dead'.

Pelé, Georgie Best, Garrincha. Three who played football for the very love of playing. Three who were caught up in fame – and the last two dealt with it worse than the first. But wonderful movers each of them. If I were the Grey I would take you to see them. As it is, you will have to use your own imagination. I will try to tell you how they moved and you will try to see them in your mind's eye.

Did you see them?

I saw clips of them.

Clips?

I am old, Kell, I saw them on the Net. And more importantly I have mirrored their motion in my mind. I have learnt from them how to play football. Pelé could halt his motion and at the very moment the defender stopped his, Pelé would be away. Bestie knew just how close to take the ball to a defender; not too close to be tackled and not so far away but that the defender felt he had to commit himself to a tackle. George just slid off tackles, his technique wasn't premeditated, he responded to the defenders' movements – he danced with them ... one, two, three players left in his wake. I learnt their secret. It was the same as Matthews'. The defenders were looking at their feet but they were balanced in the heart.

She made a sudden swift movement and poked her finger into my chest, slightly to the right of centre on the same level as my heart. She held and pressed her finger there for a moment so I could feel the place.

There! She said, *There is the balance point, the centre of motion, the impulse-giver of your movement.*

She was silent for a time. My gaze was caught by the drawings of the footballers. I imagined them to be moving or did I really see them in motion.

After the evening meal she put three ground-nut tree-syrup sweets on the table, they had the shapes of the footballers. I thought of them as Pelé, Garrincha and Bestie. She was telling me about football: Tactics, history, the players. I let her talk. I only understood about a third of what she was saying but I pictured the football being played in my mind. She told me that all the nations had their star players. Argentina for instance had De Stefano, Maradona and Messi. She said that football helped channel the instincts of the warrior into play, that football helped weaken what she called 'the Shire mentality' and brought about a widening of awareness, national and international consciousness without nations waging war against each other. And above all that children learnt to play with their fellows while enhancing friendship and the sense for fair play.

We were outside on an evening walk when I asked if Pelé, George and Garrincha were the best of all the footballers.

She was mute for a moment before answering, *Well there was Messi, but my favourite is Duncan, Duncan Edwards. Bobby Charlton, who was a fine player in his own right, was in no doubt. He played against Pelé and against Garrincha at their best, he played against Beckenbauer, he played every week with George Best at their club just as he had earlier played every week with Duncan. Charlton was in no doubt: "Duncan Edwards was the best player he ever saw and ever would see". Duncan died when he was only 21. He was killed with a number of other fine players in a plane crash.*

A plane?

She ruffled my hair, *Oh Kell, you have such a lot to learn. I only hope I am not going too far and too fast for you.*

I opened my door, she was looking off into the distance, *Would that the Grey were here*, she whispered to herself.

As I was lying in bed and she sitting on the bed holding my hand, she spoke again, *Had Duncan lived he might have played every week with Georgie Best. Best would have learnt from him and he from George. Pelé and Garrincha would have learnt from Duncan and he from them ... and maybe football would have been a nobler game.*

It was raining heavily outside as we were eating breakfast. She was taciturn having said nothing to me but 'Good morning'. I looked up at the shelf with the ground-nut sweets of footballers. There were only two left. I had gobbled up Garrincha for last night's desert. She was shaping marzipan.

Duncan? I said as she stood up and placed it beside Pelé and Bestie.

In the posture of the statue they made of him in his home town of Dudley.

Was Duncan the best sportsman ever?

She laughed heartily and long as I had ever heard her laugh, *Oh Kell, it's not the football they played on earth, it's the football they take with them into the heavens which really matters.* Her face became more serious, *But to answer your question, I can think of at least two who were as good.* She went to a chest and took out a red leather ball which fitted into her hand and two wooden bats, one of which was small enough for me. I found out a bit later they were called cricket bats. *Was anyone ever better than Leonardo, Michaelangelo or Raphael at putting the human figure onto canvas? Did any sport ever reach the zenith of cricket as it was before the First World War? With W. G. Grace, Ranji Singh, George Lohmann, Tom Richardson, Sidney Barnes, Fred Spofforth, Charlie Macartney, Victor and Jack. Victor Trumper and Jack Hobbs perhaps the best batsmen ever.*

She looked out of the window, *It's raining – just the weather for* not *playing cricket. Now I'll tell you about the rules of cricket. Easy enough, a couple of hours should suffice.*

Monika could talk as fast as she could move if she were animated. She got me to hold a bat and described bowling. I saw before my inner sight the fast bowler Tom

Richardson running in to bowl. I held the bat, she guided my posture and my movement. I tried to drive off the back foot, hook and cut. Then I tried to drive off the front foot and cracked the bat against my ankle. It took all my effort not to burst into tears.

I sat down and watched as she with effortless grace cut, drove, hooked and then glided an imaginary ball down to Fine Leg. I heard about how Sidney Barnes learnt to spin the ball viciously even while bowling at fast medium pace. She told me how she had learnt his secret regarding the release of the ball so that it spun with a whirr not by turning the ball with the fingers as an off-spinner does but by having the ball rip from his grip.

You have already learnt that technique, Kell, when swerving the ball around staves. With a real cricket ball it will not only swing in the air, it will also spin off the ground. Barnes got the ball to swerve into the right-handed batsman and once it pitched, it spun away – at fast medium pace! He used to practise using the very same technique as we practised only he used stumps instead of staves. He bent it around one stump, an in-swinging swerve, then got it to pitch and spin back to the offside. Are you following?

She didn't give me time to answer, she was putting cutlery on the table to represent the stumps and showing me how he got the ball to glide in and spin back.

Macartney, one of the very greatest batsmen, said that he was standing at the non-striking end when Barnes bowled Victor with a ball 'the batsman sees when he's tight'. That was how he put it. 'Tight' meaning under the influence of alcohol.

Alcohol?

Strong drink, like what Dung had when he thought he could become king of the hamlet. People under such influence see neither themselves nor their surroundings aright.

Did Victor take strong drink?

She smiled, *No, it was Barnes who made the ball swerve and spin so wickedly as to seem unbelievable to one who is sober. Sidney Barnes was a 'writer', which is to say, he drew letters on paper. He was concentrated on the very movement of making the forms of letters he copied onto paper or parchment like a scribe in the Egyptian Mysteries That was his job, cricket was only a weekend pastime for him. To see Victor or Jack move – that was wonderful indeed. The Grey took me to see them both.*

She gazed away into the distance as she sat there at the table, I guess she was reliving those moments of actually seeing the two batsmen from inside the memory of the world.

She turned and looked at me keenly, *The footballers tended to think their balance point was in their hips or their guts, unlike Pelé or Bestie who moved from the heart. The cricketers tended to think their balance point was in the head. Keep the head still, they used to say. They would push forward or back with the foot, lift the bat, hit the ball. Unconsciously the head was the centre of their awareness. But to see Victor lift his foot and his bat in one motion – they said, he didn't seem to watch the ball, it was almost as though he divined what the ball would do. This means he saw the space and the whole curve of the ball at one go. There is even a photograph of him with his leg and bat lifted together, the heart was the impulse giver of his movements. They would bowl a yorker at him and he would 'draw' it through his legs for four. Later batsmen couldn't even do the draw! And Jack hitting hundreds on good or bad wickets even against the bowling of Sidney Barnes!* She jumped up speaking very animatedly, *They say great batsmen have time to spare. This is because they are living the future in the now. Do you understand, Kell? No, of course not, I am just an old woman waxing lyrical, as the commentators used to say, about the joys of cricket.*

She sat down again and looked at me fondly, the tone of her voice becoming more matter of fact, *Football and cricket widened people's perspectives. One town against another, one county against another, one country against another – not a war, a game! And children playing, concentrating, moving, playing.* She cupped her chin in the palms of her hands as she continued, *Football was for the working class. Cricket for all the classes, the rich and the poor played on equal terms: Gentlemen against Players. One humanity, one earth. How I love sports, Kell.*

And I loved to listen to her when she spoke with such life and verve, it didn't even matter if I only understood a quarter of what she was telling me. But by then I was bursting to move myself. *Monika, I think it's stopped raining.*

Then to bat and ball, today is a day of play – only I have to get you a box if we are to play cricket.

Do we play cricket in a box? I pictured myself bowling against Victor inside a huge wooden box.

Not that kind of box, er, more of a thing, well, something to protect what's between your legs.

Oh! I pictured Sid bowling at me, the bright red ball viciously biting the ground and rising into my … I was lying on the ground wailing and writhing in agony.

What on earth are you doing? She was looking down at me with her mouth open.

I tried to get up, I was on all fours as I glanced up at her, *I, er, took Barnes' ball, well, between the legs.*

30. Sport Fall

Next morning as I sat sipping a special treat, black tea with dried milk, I glanced up at the shelf. Last evening I had been ravenously hungry and had eaten both Pelé and Best. Duncan was by himself in full flow and about to fire the ball. Monika was making another ground-nut syrup sweet in the image of Victor Trumper with lifted leg and lifted bat seeing the whole curve of the ball without seeming to look at it.

She sat down beside me with her cup of green tea and placed Victor on the table. *Ah, Kell, I have spoken to you about the joy of sport, and the joys are real but I would be giving you a one-sided and thus a false picture if I did not describe how Falarch intentions as a kind of disease became entwined into its bones. Sport underwent corruption on almost every level*. She folded her arms, *What can one say? Man fell. And everything we do is cast in shadow.* She gave an audible sigh, *Falarch power was felt above all in finance, in money.*

Money?

Oh, Kell, at least you are safe from that. What a joy not to know about monetary power. But, she paused as though not quite knowing how to carry on.

I looked at Duncan on the shelf and Victor on the table, and resolved not to eat them. I got a start when her voice rang out into the room.

Rewards, top players were given rewards. Money, fame, adulation, women – anything they wanted. And the sports stars thought their own abilities won matches. Bah! The cripple, the aged person, the stroke victim, all know better. To be able to move at all is an act of grace. Do you know what happens in your blood and in your muscles when you lift your arm? Do you consciously set sugars in your cells to burn to create energy?

Once by accident I had dropped a clump of raw sugar into a fire. How brightly it had burnt. I was imagining fires burning inside my arm as I lifted it up.

Do you know, Kell? No, you don't. Not even the Grey knows that. But top sports stars of yesteryear puffed out their chests believing themselves to be great. And only results were considered important. The Falarch-controlled media preached that winning mattered not playing. Yet what trophy, what prize money can compare to being able to run, to walk, to stand – to being able to move at all?

She stood up sipping tea from her cup as she stepped to the window, *They controlled organisations which bore down right into children's play, 'Play by system!', 'Winning counts!', 'Win by foul play if you can get away with it!'* She turned toward me, sadness in her eyes, *When knights in the Middle Ages broke their codes of conduct just for the sake of winning, they were laying the germs for social diseases which centuries later were used by Falarch forces to make sport fall short of its innocent promise*. She sat down again and looked at me steadily, *Play, Kell, for the sake of being able to play. Pride in your own achievements is false for you cannot move your body at all without help from above. And false pride is precisely what the False Architects, the Falarchs, employ to dirty our world.*

I was loosing track yet her words had such an earnestness as to keep me partially focused. I knew architects design buildings and I found myself picturing homes made from living materials: Wood, stone, earth, with grass roofs and with people playing football or cricket or fondling their pets. But beside these dwellings were other ugly buildings constructed from grey blocks and between them were slaves, all dressed alike, carrying fat and cagey Falarchs in carriages borne on their shoulders while spliced rats scurried round their boots.

And sportswomen, too often feeble imitators of men. A woman's etheric is more vibrant than a man's, and through the etheric our limbs are brought into movement. Women tennis players standing at the back of the court trying to emulate male fire-power, yet never realising their own finer ethereal forces allow them to form more fluid strokes. Think of Ahwenda–

That was easy. I saw her in my imagination running with a football at her feet, dancing around Dung-like defenders to lob the ball neatly over the keeper's head. I thought of myself passing the ball back and forth with her between big and bulky opponents.

I must have drifted clean away because she almost shouted my name, *Kell, think how Ahwenda can move with smooth flow faster than men.*

I pictured Ahwenda in full flight outstripping blundering Dung-males who were out of breath, lumbering and slobbering in her wake.

Monika put her hand on my shoulder as she spoke, *But let us not bother about Falarch malfeasance–*

I seemed to remember the word 'feces' meaning, well, what we push out of our back ends. In my mind's eye I saw a line of big, greasy, crafty Falarchs with trousers round their ankles bending over and grunting as they did their businesses while spliced boars waited greedily behind them to breakfast on fresh Falarch feces.

Come, Kell, playtime. Football this morning and cricket, if it doesn't rain, this afternoon.

31. Letters, Numbers, Forms and Flowers

Summer disappears swiftly in the North once the darkness of night returns. Yet those seven of eight weeks before Autumn really set in were some of the most contented in my childhood. We received word that Maria had reached the place where she was to live. And though I missed my little sister sorely, I was so glad she was safe.

In the mornings we had school. Monika told me stories. And from out of a story we would draw a picture, then simplify the picture, simplify it again until it became a letter. She said she was following Stoner's curriculum.

She made me draw letters in sand and model them in clay. She made me lie on my back and draw letters in the air with my feet. She also got me doing 'form movement' in the eurythmy hall. We drew an imaginary line down the centre of the hall and she would move in toward the line and away from it, sometimes in rounded movements, sometimes in pointed ones. I had to move a so as to keep the symmetry.

We would start standing at the same distance from this imaginary line, me on the right of it, she on the left. If she moved forward, I had to move forward to keep level with her; if she moved toward the line, I moved toward it; if she moved away from it, I did too. Always trying to move in the same way as Monika, always seeking to maintain the symmetry with the imaginary line in the middle between us.

Again and again she would say, *The heart, we draw the forms with our hearts, our feet follow the heart*. And she would stop me from running. *Walk, Kell, walk! Always keep at least one part of one foot on the ground*.

I was dissatisfied with this at first. She could walk fast, much quicker than me. I would moan, *I can only keep up if I run.*

Bolloc– she started to say. Then shaking her head she pointed to the window and said to me, *Do you remember Djorki chasing Ahwenda and the Grey?*

I followed the direction of her arm and recalled vividly in my mind Ahwenda running swift as a deer and the Grey beside her.

What was the Grey doing?

Running.

Was he now? Look again.

I searched my memory carefully: His feet were moving as quickly as I could wave may arm back and forth but he wasn't running – he was walking! The Grey could walk as fast as Ahwenda could run! I looked up at her with my mouth open.

Yes, your heart moves forward, your feet follow – as rapidly as a bird can beat its wings if need be. And remember, when you walk you don't tire.

Sometimes she would stand shoulder to shoulder with me, well, my shoulder nearly up to her elbow, and she would make a downward form with her left hand and I was to do a symmetry form with my right hand. After this she would get me to do the movement, she had made, with my left hand while simultaneously keeping the symmetry with my right hand, my own upright being the axis of symmetry.

Then she would get me to lie on my back, lift my legs and do the same symmetrical form with my right and left legs together.

Learn to love forms, Kell, And numbers!

I had always liked numbers and often counted things or just counted to a hundred for fun. Monika made me say: 1, 2, 3 – with one and two spoken quietly and three loudly. 1, 2, <u>3</u>, 4, 5, <u>6</u>, 7, 8, <u>9</u> – putting the beat on every third number. Then she got me to say the first two numbers in the sequence silently inside me while every third number was spoken aloud, so that I said: 3, 6, 9, 12, 15, 18, 21, 24, 27, 30 – the three times table! She also got the times table right down into my legs by taking two little steps followed by a longer stride on the third.

In this way I learnt the tables.

She seemed very pleased with me, *You have a knack for numbers. But numbers are not only ordinal they are cardinal. Thus three is not only the natural number after two and before four, the number three has a quality in its own right. Are you following?*

Er?

How many leaves does a clover have?

Er?

Go and find one.

I went outside a picked a clover, it had three leaves. All the clovers had three leaves.

When I came back in she posed me a problem, she put an apple in my hand and asked me to find the five-pointed star in it. I looked all around it, from the top and from the bottom but couldn't see any star shape.

She handed me a knife, *Cut it in two. No, not from top to bottom, cut across.*

When I cut across it, the five-pointed star revealed itself.

How many petals does an apple blossom have?

Five perhaps?

She nodded. *Now go outside for half an hour, Kell, and look at flowers. Count the number of petals on each flower – and open your palm to them.*

That half an hour passed very quickly. I saw how some flowers had four, some five and some six petals. Some had even more but Monika told me these were composite flowers, where the flower itself was made up of a number of smaller flowers.

When I came in, she had replaced the picture of the Magician by that of the High Priestess.

The second of the Major Arcana. There are twenty two in all. In time you will learn about each of the twenty-two qualities. The Magician is oneness, the Priestess is reflection, twoness. She pointed at a branch on the table, *Look at that, what number do you find in it*?

It was mistletoe – it was twoness.

The sun shines out of itself, it is one. The moon shines because it reflects the light of the sun, it is two. Forms, numbers, letters – vowels and consonants – and words live behind the physical, the etheric, the astral and the higher worlds. She picked up the mistletoe and twirled it, *Numbers hide and reveal at the same time just as the Arcana hide and reveal. We have to thank Mountain for making this plain to us*.

Filosopsy again! I glanced up at Duncan and Victor on the shelf, *Monika, can I have a desert?*

I have something special for you. Take a look, she pointed at an iron saucepan.

I grabbed a stool so I could stand on it and peer into the saucepan. There was a dark brown liquid in it. *What is it?*

Hot chocolate – well, cocoa, cocoa butter, vanilla, malt syrup, dark sugar and milk.

My first taste of hot chocolate! I tried to lick out the very last drop with my tongue.

I enjoyed schooling – letters, numbers, forms – but I enjoyed play-practice even more. We played football and cricket. Mainly football because our cricket wicket was a bit too bumpy. She got me to bowl to her but wouldn't let me face her bowling on the uneven pitch. Instead I had to practise imaginary shots with my bat: Drives off the front and the back foot, cuts, hooks, leg glances and sweeps. My left ankle was sore as I sometimes hit it with the bat when I was driving off the front foot.

32. Old Versus Young

Monika had said I had a talent for numbers and for football. I began to practise times tables by juggling with a football. One and two low, and on every third kick I would send the ball up to the level of my head for the three times table. I would also do this table running with a ball; one, two steps forward and a body swerve on the third.

She told me, we couldn't make a real football filled with air as they used to. Ours was filled with uncombed wool. This made it easier to juggle but it didn't bounce much at all. She got me making these wool-stuffed balls.

Get right into the football, Kell, make it yours. Stitch it together, fill it with wool, learn everything about it.

After six weeks of football practice I was amazed at how much I'd improved. Throwing had been tough but football was sheer joy.

Dungbjorn had been away, I don't know where. He came back one afternoon and saw me running with a football at my feet.

Football! he shouted, *Dung love football. Come try dribble Dung.*

I approached him with the ball at my feet imagining Stanley Matthews, and Bestie – close but not too close, and Messi so naturally adjusting the length of his strides so as to be able to attack the leg which bore the defenders weight. Dungbjorn was big but when he lifted one of his legs, I immediately swerved toward his other leg and past him – or almost. Mutty was too quick, his nose took the ball off my toe and I tumbled full length over him. Djorki let out a bark and was in the skirmish. The two dogs were biting the ball and pulling against each other, uncombed wool was falling out of the ball.

It would take me a couple of days to make another if Monika didn't help. I glanced up and saw her striding toward us. Djorki let go of the ball and hung his head guiltily but Mutty ran off with the ball in his mouth in triumph.

Dungbjorn, what is the meaning–

Football, football! Monika boy playing football! He pointed at me, my nose was still in the dirt, pure joy shone from his face.

The sternness in her features dissolved, she seemed to be suppressing a smile, *Come, Kell, we have to make another ball.*

By early evening we were finished. Monika was sitting quietly in a chair with folded hands and eyes closed. I was left to juggle with another ball much smaller than the one we used outside. All at once she opened her eyes wide and sat up straight, motioning me to stop.

Anything wrong?

Shush!

Very still she sat, poised as if she were a spring waiting to uncoil. A passing smile crossed her face and although she seemed to maintain the same posture, I could see she had relaxed.

A minute later there was a soft tap on the door.

Open it Kell.

A little apprehensively I unlatched the door. A hooded figure stood before me. I gasped and retreated. As the figure stepped quickly inside and bent toward me, I fell over backwards.

What no kiss for a wanderer from the night? throwing back her hood Ahwenda knelt before me smiling.

We were eating breakfast next morning when there was a

loud knock on the door. Ahwenda opened. Dungbjorn peered in, *Monika play football with Dung?*

This time Monika wasn't able to suppress a smile, *Mr. Dungbjorn–*

Couldn't we, Monika? Ahwenda interrupted, *I haven't played football for years*.

I joined in the plea. It was three against one.

Half an hour later we were on the lawn ready to play. Many of the villagers stood around waiting for the game to start. Dung had been shouting his mouth off about playing football with Monika. Looking back I think most of the men came just to see Ahwenda. Both she and Monika wore tight fitting clothes and pony tails. Dung wore his usual bear skins. Sides were soon agreed, old versus young. Me and Ahwenda were to play together.

Dung banged his chest with a huge fist, *Me play with Monika!*

It was a strange match. Monika insisted on the pitch being fairly small, *So skill rather than speed decide*.

She played in defence. Dung blundered around trying to tackle us while she waited to pounce. Ahwenda would happily run around Dung but she seemed to hold back when facing Monika. Maybe I could have dribbled Dung but he was big so I had to run wide to get past him. And if I put the ball through his legs I might just as well have passed to Monika for she just collected the ball. Me and Dung were certainly trying, especially Dung. Ahwenda told me not to tackle Dung as he might fall on top of me. She seemed to be trying too unless she confronted Monika one on one.

We ended up passing to each other. Dung would run at me, I would slip the ball to Ahwenda and she would drift forward, the ball seemed to be attached to her feet. When Monika stood before her she would slip the ball back to me. And I would try to shoot or pass back to her. If I shot on target I generally scored. If we passed more than three times Monika invariably intercepted the ball. I got the feeling it was okay to pass but any attempts to humiliate the big man would be scotched by Monika's intercepting.

If Monika had the ball she would move forward, I might have said 'darted forward' only her movements were so smooth and fluid, and passed to Dung who was free to shoot. Sometimes he shot on target, sometimes wide and sometimes he missed the ball all together. We won the first game 6–5.

In the second game it was 5–4 to us when Monika passed to Dung he took a mighty kick at it and completely missed but somehow she managed to collect her own pass, shouting, *Fine decoy, Dungbjorn*, as she cannoned the ball into goal. 5 all.

Ahwenda scored the winning goal. She had set me free, I shot but the ball screwed upwards off my foot, she leapt into the air, her body was parallel to the ground at shoulder height as she scissor-kicked the ball into goal. 6–5.

We won the third game 6–5 as well. Even I began to feel there was something funny about this. I'm not sure if Dung could count so he didn't seem to notice the score, he just moaned about losing three games in a row.

As we were walking off I noted how small Monika was. Dung was big and broad, she was tiny. On the pitch it was different. You kind of felt her presence at the back as huge. Wherever she needed to be, she was. But once the game was over, you hardly noticed her.

We played again next day. Walking onto the pitch, I asked Monika, *How come we won all the games 6–5.*

Her only comment was, *Mm.*

The whole village seemed to have turned out to watch.

Many of the men were talking animatedly about Ahwenda. I heard her name spoken a lot as we were warming up. Just before we kicked off, I took her arm and said under my breath, *You are so quick, you should take Monika on and go past her.*

The morning belonged to Ahwenda. She went at Monika at full pace swerving by her and scoring on two or three occasions. And what I hadn't seen before was how wonderful a goalkeeper she was. It was almost as though she had been holding back on the first day. When Monika passed to Dung, with three strides and in the twinkling of an eye Ahwenda would be back between the goal posts so when he shot, she was there to pluck the ball out of the air or turn it round the post. We won the first game 6–2 and the second 6–1.

Just before the start of the third game I saw Monika grab Ahwenda by the arm and whisper something to her urgently.

Inspired by Ahwenda's speed and freedom, I took on Dung successfully twice. 3–1 to us. The character of the game had changed though, both Ahwenda and Monika seemed to be holding back.

At one point Dung got the ball and charged forward, I was between him and our goal. Somehow he managed to trip over the ball and fall headlong forward. I could see his face tumbling toward mine. His nose was only a couple of inches from my forehead when his body just seemed to stop in mid air. Monika held him up by one shoulder and Ahwenda by the other. His nose would have been crushed and my head shoved down my neck if they hadn't caught him.

We were both shocked by what had happened. The game was stopped. Dung went home with his dog. We three went back to drink strong black tea. I was given a spoonful of honey in mine. My body was trembling when Monika went out.

I turned to Ahwenda, *How did, how was it possible?*

There was a tear in her eye as she replied, *I am shaking too, Kell.*

Yeah, Dung's heavy.

It's not that, it's ... well, if danger threatens, there are certain signs. Monika noticed them. We didn't know what was going to happen but we were on our guard. The moment he fell, we knew – and we were just able to get there in time.

She reached out to me and I fell into her arms. We were both crying.

And we were still in tears when Monika returned. She sat down and poured herself another cup of tea, *Nothing like a good cup of tea after a shock.*

Ahwenda wiped her eyes with her sleeve, *I'm sorry, I–*

No need for that. Dung's crying too, like a baby. He wouldn't let me in when I went to see him. She drained her cup and gave us that unfathomable Monika look, *I think we have just been witness to the untying of a karmic knot.* After another pause she added, *No more sniffling, this is not the time, I want us all back on the pitch in half an hour.*

Half an hour later we were ready. I felt much better after the cry. Dung was still a bit subdued. The game began as the first two of this day with Ahwenda flying through gaps or weaving past Monika or bounding back to block Dung's shots. 4–0 to us.

Dung came back to life, *Monika we lost every game.*

Mm, was her only comment.

The villagers were shouting, *Ahwenda, Ahwenda!*

She couldn't help breaking into a smile as they chanted her name.

I got the ball ran forward made as if to pass to Ahwenda, noticed how Dung moved across to cover her and swerved away from him. Ahwenda ran into space, I pushed the ball perfectly into her path ... and she was tumbling forward. Monika had taken the ball off her toe with a left-footed sliding tackle.

It's been years since I slide tackled, she said as she took Ahwenda's hand to lift her up.

The character of the game totally altered. When Ahwenda went to take on Monika, I saw how they were a little closer. It was almost as though everything was slowing down for me. I became aware of processes behind their movements. As Monika had so often exhorted me, I became conscious of their hearts, the centres of their chests. As Ahwenda sought to dance past her, Monika seemed to be able to link their hearts, her steps were small and blindingly fast, she would take the ball from Ahwenda, sometimes with a slide tackle, more often than not though she just took it away from her and passed to Dung.

Most of the time Ahwenda was able to bound back and block his shots. At 4–3 Ahwenda passed to me, I was free and fired the ball in, 5–3 to us. That was the last goal we scored.

Monika didn't release the ball at once to Dung next time she had it. Ahwenda in goal, Monika running forward and with hardly any noticeable backlift she sent the ball past her. This happened twice. The third time she took a slightly higher back lift, Ahwenda dived, Monika slipped the ball sideways for Dung to tap in. He shouted and jumped for joy. The villagers went quiet.

'Nother game, another game, he roared.

Last match, said Monika.

We lost 6–0.

Ahwenda was completely at a loss when she tried to

take Monika on. And even when she tried to pass to me Monika seemed to be able to intercept or be able to deftly block my shots. I had the distinct impression that if Ahwenda's footballing ability was represented by her size and she were normal sized, then Monika was a giant, while me and Dung were tiny, tiny midgets.

Monika began to take on Ahwenda and it was Ahwenda who floundered, if not quite in a Dung-like at least in a lady-like fashion she floundered.

Monika was doing the Pelé-thing, she moved quickly forward and as Ahwenda came in to take her, she stopped and just at the instant Ahwenda stopped, Monika darted forward leaving Ahwenda in her wake. I tried to watch their chests, Ahwenda's motion didn't seem to have form. But when Monika brought her movement to a stop, it seemed as though the centre of her chest made a tiny circular motion, flying forward again just as Ahwenda stopped.

At one point Ahwenda came across to block her but Monika slipped the ball between Ahwenda's legs with her left foot and as Ahwenda turned swiftly to take her on again, Monika put the ball back between Ahwenda's legs with her right foot. Ahwenda lost balance and ended on her bottom.

Monika looked down at her and said, *I saw Pelé do that once and have always wanted to try it*.

As I ran to take her on, she casually flicked the ball over my head for Dung to put the ball into an empty goal. 4–0.

Next time she ran toward goal, Ahwenda flew at her. Monika didn't do anything tricky, she drifted slightly toward her so their shoulders met. Ahwenda let out something between a shriek and a shout as she tumbled sideways head over heels and came to a sitting position.

All right? asked Monika.

Was that legal? Ahwenda was smiling.

Perfectly.

The ball was behind Monika, I rushed over to take it. A split second before I got there, she back-heeled the ball into goal, 5–0.

The last goal was also memorable. I had tried to pass to Ahwenda between Dung's legs. Monika intercepted. Ahwenda didn't try to tackle her, she went flying back to defend our goal. Monika lofted the ball over her head. But Ahwenda was quick, three paces from our goal line she leapt high into the air to catch the ball.

Then something strange happened. The ball began to spin and instead of falling into Ahwenda's outstretched hands it remained hovering, almost suspended in mid air. As she landed back on the ground, the ball looped over her into the goal.

Ahwenda could hardly stop laughing as she pointed at Monika and said, *That was definitely not legal.*

Monika put her finger to her lips.

Dung was roaring, *Monika and Dung won! We won! Monika wizard.*

One of the women in the hamlet pointed at her hissing, *The old witch!*

I didn't care, Ahwenda had been treated to a footballing master class and I had been lucky enough to witness it.

Dung lifted Monika onto his shoulders as he shouted, *Monika champion, Monika champion!*

33. The Outside Closes In

Late that same afternoon the wind began blowing, clouds billowed up from the South darkening the sky. Monika spent almost half an hour gazing up at the heavens as though perceiving more than weather patterns.

Night drew around the hamlet, rain lashed the window panes. We sat subdued by the fire. Monika had a book on her lap but she seemed to be thinking rather than reading. Ahwenda sat crosslegged on the floor. No mention was made of football, sport or play-practice. We hardly spoke at all. Monika had made ground nut syrup sweets of Messi and Jack Hobbs to set beside Victor and Duncan. I felt a bit guilty about having guzzled Garrincha, Pelé and George Best.

Wind rattled the shutters. The outside, cold and shorn of light, was closing in around our home. I nestled up against Ahwenda, she put her arms round me and started to hum a song. Still none of us spoke. I must have fallen asleep for I was woken by a loud knock. Monika might have been waiting by the door for she was opening it even as I glanced up. She stood gazing into the darkness beyond the threshold. A sudden gust of wind blew out two of the candles. My heart beat rapidly as she retreated from the doorway and allowed him to enter. Casting back his hood he winked at Ahwenda and put his arms out for me. I scrambled up and ran to him.

The impetuous seven year old pre-empted adult conversation, I began yapping to him about football, cricket and about the match with Dung.

A good job, said the Grey, *That ladies were present when you tussled with the big fellow.*

I saw again Dung's nose stopping and inch or two from my forehead and shivered.

Monika was making a hot drink. He sat in a chair in front of the flames with me on his lap and Ahwenda at his feet, *Are they?* she asked looking at him, her blue eyes clouded with concern.

He nodded, *But not today or tomorrow.* He ruffled my hair, *So how many times can you juggle the ball?*

Twelve, I answered proudly, *And when you come next time I will have reached a hundred.*

Some time later as I began drifting toward a deep untroubled slumber, I felt them lift me and lay me on a fleece near the wall opposite the door.

It was early morning and still completely dark when from great heights and forgetfulness I felt my myself drawn to consciousness. I became aware of the Grey One speaking to me but couldn't to recognise where I was. I stared up into his face, a single candle lit the room. He was fully clothed as was Ahwenda who stood behind his kneeling form.

I am sorry to wake you little one but we are leaving now and I am not sure when we will return.

I clasped his hand and closed my eyes, his voice bore me back to the womb of dreamless sleep.

The sun had risen but the rain still fell heavily outside. It was late when I joined her at the breakfast table. Here in Monika's home his absence left me with an intangible ache.

It rained for two more days almost non-stop. We didn't go outside. She had meals brought to us. Much of the time she spent going through her belongings, sorting them out and putting them into bags. *How much one accumulates! And sooner or later it all has to be left behind.*

I had nothing except my calling stone. The little lamb, I

had slept with, had gone with my sister.

Hours were spent with my nose at the window watching rain drops trickle down the glass. How I longed to go out and play football or cricket. Yet more than anything I wished I could leave the hamlet and travel with him.

Around noon on the third day since their departure the clouds broke and the sun peeped through. The ground was too soggy to play on. That afternoon she had me try on new warm Winter clothes and changed the stitching so they fitted me properly.

As I lay on my bed that evening holding her hand, I didn't want her to leave. I couldn't bring myself to bring Kaspar to mind. I just wanted her to stay and sing to me until sleep enveloped me.

She made as if to rise, I held tightly onto her hand, *Monika, where do we come from?*

She gazed down at me, making no move either to leave or to answer.

Where do I come from?

There, she answered poking me slightly to the right of the centre of my chest, *There you come from, or maybe I should say, there you come through*.

She slipped my hand and stood up. I sensed she had many pressing things to do but I didn't want her to go.

As she put her finger to the latch I asked, *Why am I me?*

Her glance was searching, *That is a question we all ask ourselves, little one*. Just as she was closing the door she added, *Keep asking, Kell. Put your fingers on that special place slightly to the right of the heart and ask the question*.

The door closed behind her. I set both my hands upon that special place and spoke aloud, *Who am I?*

An emptiness bore me away from my childhood, I

sensed in that instant my enigmatic grown-up self stir and approach me from a time yet to be.

It was too much, I didn't want to be grown up, not yet. I called Kaspar's name aloud, closed my eyes and allowed myself to be in the lonely yet strangely comforting presence of his unlit cell.

Next day I felt completely lost. Monika had many visitors: guards and Rangemen. She called a meeting of the villagers. There was no place for me. I felt I didn't belong.

Where did I belong? The question came to me but not the answer.

Not even ball juggling appealed to me. I missed my little sister sorely and wondered if she missed me or whether there was no place for me in her new life with the Seeresses across the seas.

Whatever seas were – water never seeming to cease, they said.

And all day my sense of not belonging never seemed to cease.

I became aware of a time yet to be, my future self stirred, no longer quite content to wait peacefully for me to grow up. Yet I wished I didn't have to grow up. I wished I could remain a child for a long, long stretch of days.

For I knew – I don't know how – that the future would cause time to speed up and roll away the nature of the carefree child into adult cares and endless, endless chores.

Monika must have been alerted to my sense of being lost because she sat beside me on my bed singing, singing in Russian, German, English, French, Italian and Swedish … until finally I fell asleep.

34. Zigzagging

The next day my childhood quietly returned. I was no longer bothered about the visitors and the goings on. I wandered around the village and looked at everything: trees, plants, the washing hut, the five thresholds of the hamlet and let myself relive many of the events that had happened to me during my life.

That evening as I lay snugly in my bed remembering that first time I entered my own little dwelling with the Grey One, I heard the connecting panel being removed. Monika spoke quietly, *Kell get dressed and come in to me.*

I fumbled to light a candle and dress in the cold. I put on my new warm winter clothes and for some reason put my calling stone into a pocket of the coat. As I opened my door the frost-filled night froze my face. The waxing moon bore a bluish sheen, a bright star shone near it.

Fire was blazing in her hearth, I stumbled toward it putting my hands out to warm them. There were no lights in the room except that which came from the fire. I knelt on the hearth rug and gazed at the flames.

Am I not worth a greeting?

I glanced to my right, Ahwenda sat on a low chair, her grey cloak folded about her. The firelight danced in her smiling face.

Kell, will you go with Ahwenda to visit the Rangemen?

I turned to Monika and nodded eagerly.

Then you will need to sleep, as you must depart with the dawn.

She took my hand even before she finished speaking and drew me to where skins lay on the floor further away from the fire. I settled down fully clothed. It felt very pleasant to be in Monika's home, I lay on my side, the two women sat in low chairs on either side of the fire whispering together. Pictures of Rangemen, camp fires and calling stones filled my mind and wove into my dreams.

In the middle of the night I woke abruptly and stared at Monika who was standing, wringing her hands and no longer speaking in whispers.

You will marry – but why, why so young? Will you not wait? After a short pause she continued, *My child, he is so young and inexperienced and–*

Ahwenda rose from the chair and knelt gazing up at the older woman, *Will you not give your blessing, it would mean so much?*

She looked down at Ahwenda's face gleaming in the glow of the fire and stroked her hair.

Will you not give your blessing ... to both of us?

Monika turned away and put a hand to her forehead as though choking back tears and moved away from the fire. Ahwenda was left kneeling on the hearth rug, her head sank.

I awoke with a chill wind in my face. Above me stars twinkled. I was outside and knew from the scent borne on the breezes that we were not in the hamlet. Lifting myself up on my elbow I noticed two figures a few feet from me. By their voices I recognised them as Monika and Ahwenda.

For your sake, my child, I will lift all curses even those harboured unconsciously. As for blessings – let an old woman weep a while longer and we shall see. But always, Ahwenda, I will bless you and your children born or unborn.

They clasped each other. As they let their embrace slip, she spoke again, *You must leave before light. I have seen their carrion birds. The hawks are few and no longer attack the spliced filth. Better you were far from here when the sun shines upon the good and the evil.*

And you, will the hamlet be safe if the Hordes advance?

In answer Monika pointed at a nearby bush, a shaft of fire shot forth as though from her fingertip, the bush crackled into flame. *I have been practising,* she said as she took a small object from an inner pocket and placed it in Ahwenda's hand, *The twin stone is worn upon my breast.*

Ahwenda kissed her on either cheek.

A sob came into Monika's voice, *Go, go now, but remember to take you little bundle.* She waved her arm toward me.

I shut my eyes and pretended to be asleep. A moment later I felt myself being lifted, Ahwenda's delicate fragrance was about me. We moved away smoothly. When I opened my eyes but a moment or two later there was already some distance between us and Monika. She stood beside the bush which was still in flame. Djorki was with her, she leant toward him and seemed to speak to him.

She lifted her arm and a glint of silvery light filled the sky.

Monika's farewell, little one.

Her voice made me jump. I saw the whiteness of her teeth in the starlit dark as she smiled down at me. I looked back at Monika now standing alone and distant by the tiny fire.

Ahwenda's face was set in the direction we were going even as she spoke, *In bygone days they said, little boys should be seen and not heard. Perhaps nowadays we should say, little boys should sleep when they are meant to and not pretend to be asleep while listening to conversations which don't concern them.*

From the merriment in her voice I knew she wasn't angry. Unlike Monika, Ahwenda was easy to read. I snuggled up to her. The gentle sway of her movements quickly lulled me to sleep.

When I awoke the sun had long risen. We were still moving swiftly. Walking not running but her pace, even with me as baggage, matched that of a distance runner. Her features were strained though, fleet-footed as she was, she wasn't used to bearing the burden of a seven year old in her arms.

She slowed, we glided toward a fast flowing stream which cascaded down and widened out. She set me on a flat stone near the water's edge and put her hands under the falling water and drank. *It is good. Come, drink.*

I hadn't realised how thirsty I was until I started to drink the cool, fresh water. She gave me a little biscuit and told me to chew it well. It had a wholesome nutty fruit flavour. We sat side by side upon the stone, spray from the cascade filled the air, the Autumn sun shone bright, the weather was mild.

How is your throwing, little one?

Not good, I can't ball-weave.

Nor can most of those training to be Rangemen until they reach their late twenties or middle thirties. Many never learn.

I think Monika would prefer me to mop than throw, I muttered sulkily.

She gave a hearty laugh, *She had me training with the mop too. I'm sure she treated her own children to a dose of mopping.*

Does Monika have children? I stared up at her with my mouth open. I always thought of Monika as being by herself.

Ahwenda's lips tightened and she frowned. I began to recognise that this expression came to her when she felt she'd done something amiss.

How old is Monika?

Older than she looks.

I jumped up wanting to move my limbs. She sprang up beside me and started to speak again, *I saw her before. It was, well, the Grey took me. I saw her when she was much younger, when her hair streamed golden, when a warrior's splendour shone about her, when she sang – at High Meals she would sing, her voice firing the Resistance to noble deeds against the Shadow. And when she danced ...* Ahwenda stood gazing into the distance as though peering into the memories of the world before continuing, *For me she seemed only a step down from the Grey One himself. She was my heroine. She was Russian and grew up far from here in a world so different from our own. Upon the black Slavic earth it was difficult for the manipulated plants to take root, gene-spliced organisms seemed almost a Western phenomenon. There had been wars, and civilisation, such as it had been in the twentieth and for much of the twenty-first century, was no longer functioning but more than remnants remained. And there was still talk of nations and pacts between nations. The Shadow and the Light did not stand openly against each other. Monika, or Lihana as she was called then, believed in people.*

Lihana? I repeated, *I have never heard of that name.*

She believed in people – but, alas, human beings still believed they could live without angels. Her voice ended flatly. She glanced at the sky, the sun was rising to the full, *We must be moving, we have far to go before nightfall.* She slipped on her rucksack and made as if to pick me up.

Can't I walk, er, run beside you?

You can try.

After a couple of hundred paces I was out of breath and

suffering from the stitch. And she had only been walking. *Can we have a little rest?*

You can rest in my arms. In one motion she lifted me and loped away.

We went forward for hours always keeping the dark forest about half a mile to our right. Sometimes I would ask to run. She would put me down but I was only able to keep up for about a hundred yards even when she walked. On and on we went.

Where are we going?

Not so very far from here is a wood which borders the spliced forest but the trees there are not manipulated. After we have gone round that wood and only a few miles further North is another hamlet. One much closer to the Oasis of Trondheim. Rangemen will be at the hamlet and there we can find rest. Her voice sounded laboured. She could no longer run. Her face was strained.

Ahwenda, you have to rest.

Maybe. She placed me on the ground and pointed, *Over there is a waterfall which flows into pool. If the weather were warmer, we could swim*.

We walked side by side holding hands. The sound of the waterfall grew as we approached. The hills on our left had drawn closer to the dark forest. The pool was little more than a hundred yards away from its trees. She filled a drinking cup made from horn with the falling water and gave me to drink. This time we took two nutty fruit biscuits each.

Ahwenda lay on her back, *I must rest but not sleep. Stay awake Kell and watch. Five minutes and we must be off*.

I wasn't tired but fell to musing about Monika who had been Lihana. I tired picturing Monika with long flowing golden hair. Behind the sound of the waterfall though I could sense an eerie brooding. I sat up against Ahwenda, the spliced forest was close, the air chilly.

A cawing woke me, a rook flying up from the forest. Ahwenda lay fast asleep. I shivered as I tried to wake her, *Ahwenda, Ahwenda.*

Her eyes flickered and focused upon me.

I think, I may have fallen asleep too.

She glanced anxiously at the sun to ascertain its position and seemed to relax, *If you have, it can't have been for more than half an hour. But we must go.*

With me in her arms she leapt across a narrow part of the stream above the waterfall and ran on swiftly. After some minutes she glanced up at the hills and gasped. I followed the direction of her gaze and saw three dark birds circling. Ahwenda increased her pace. The birds made strange shrieking sounds which caused me to cringe and cling to her. They dived toward us. She turned right heading to the forest fleeter than a deer but the spiced birds swooped with frightening speed. The leading bird let out a vibrating bat-like screeching as it attacked. At the last moment Ahwenda veered left and only avoided its claws by inches, talons as long as my fingers and sharper than nails.

The second replicated bird attacked with a screech resembling a mosquito attack but loud as a whining wind. She was zigzagging, she swerved right but only escaped its claws by chance as her foot caught in the root of a bush and she fell headlong.

As I was jolted from her arms the change came. All my senses were heightened and everything was moving in slow motion.

The third bird swooped, its talons zooming toward her neck but I heard bounding paces and a bark. The dog's teeth snapped on the place where its wing was attached to its body. The dog's momentum carried the bird away from her. Part of its wing was ripped off.

The modified fowl tried to fly but no matter how it sought to flap its wings it could not fly properly. Djorki was standing above me. My senses returned to normal. Ahwenda was groaning.

About seventy yards away the injured bird gave up flapping and landed. The other two swooped on it. She covered my eyes with her hands. When she removed them the two birds had already killed and were making a meal of the injured one. They were ripping off great chunks of its meat and swallowing them whole. After devouring their fellow they flew up circling higher into the air and emitting their bat-like screeches. Finally they flew away South.

My shoulder hurt, I held on tightly to Ahwenda, Djorki stood beside us. Suddenly he growled. We followed his line of sight. On a hillock half a mile away we saw a wolf. Another joined it.

We must away! she scrambled to her feet even as she spoke, lifted me up and ran.

More than half a dozen wolves had gathered on the hilltop. We came over a little rise and there a few hundred yards from us was the wood she had spoken of. Golden brown leaves were still visible upon the branches of the deciduous trees. The wood bordered right up against the dark forest of manipulated fir trees.

We will make the wood ... but not the hamlet, she said half jubilantly, half resignedly.

As we entered the wood we heard a howl and saw the wolves set off loping in a line down toward us. The red sun was descending in the West.

35. Falling Branches

We had moved two or three hundred paces into the wood. It was quiet but did not have the eerie malice of the manipulated conifers. Ahwenda was breathing heavily and glancing around. I was beside her. She looked so lovely, she was so kind, good, brave, I couldn't bear the thought of her being torn apart by the canine teeth of wolves. The shocks of the journey had allowed my grown-up self to draw nearer to me.

Ahwenda go. You and Djorki can outpace the wolves. Leave me here, I can climb a tree and stay where they can't get to me.

Her eyes were moist as she looked down at me. All at once she knelt, rested her head momentarily on the ground and took my hand as she rose up on one knee, *Thank you, Kell, for freeing me from my duty.* She stood up still holding my hand and speaking almost as though the trees were witnesses, *What I do now, I do freely. You would not be safe in a tree, sooner or later sleep would overcome you and you would fall. Djorki cannot climb trees. No, we will stay together, dog, maid and boy. Together we will fight.* She raised her eyes to the deepening blue visible through the branches, *Here I will stay.*

Ahwenda, if I am to die, I would sooner die with you than anyone, though even as I spoke I thought of Monika, the Grey and perhaps most of all my little sister, Maria.

And I with you, Kell. As she spoke she glanced into the distance and I wondered if she too were thinking of Monika, the Grey One and perhaps Raynor most of all.

I buried my head into her belly, she folded her arms around me.

Even as she did, I became aware of a whistling. Someone was whistling a tune I thought I ought to know but couldn't quite recall. The whistling grew louder. Ahwenda stiffened. I turned toward the sound. Djorki was sitting on his haunches panting happily.

A man came into view. An old man to judge by his appearance, bent over with a heavy burden of branches on his back. Two of the branches seemed to be hanging loosely.

The man stopped. *Will ye no help a poor old woodcutter and put the loose branches back?* His was a country dialect and there was something strangely even thrillingly familiar about him.

I moved forward to help him. Ahwenda put her hand on my shoulder to stop me.

He repeated the question, *Will ye not aid an old woodcutter?* There was a lilt in his voice, he spoke leisurely as though he had all the time in the world.

I turned to her as I spoke, *I think we should help him*.

The dog was still quietly panting. She nodded and we stepped forward, each of us took one of the loose branches in our hands.

On second thought, he said, *Maybe ye can keep 'em. A little keepsake from the old cutter of branches*.

We both stood holding a branch as he made to move off with his burden.

With rapid speech Ahwenda began questioning him, *Where are you going? Have you a home here? Is there a safe place in these woods?*

He answered in that same leisurely tone, *Ah got far to go afore nightfall, further than ye can follow. And no, Ah got no home here, nor no home nowhere. There be no homes here, no people here in these woods*.

But wolves are after us, Ahwenda was crying as she spoke.

Wolves eh, nought worse than that eh? Well, if ye be

needing a place to hold up for a night or two, there be a wee bit of an island in the beck over there, he motioned with his hand.

We looked where he was pointing, Djorki rose to his feet and moved off in the same direction. We turned back to him. Ahwenda gasped. There was silence, no one was there. We glanced at each other in bewilderment.

Was he real? I asked.

She shook her head but still clutched the branch tightly.

The branches– I whispered.

Are real, she finished the sentence for me. *And who was he?* As she asked the question, she lifted her branch and thrust it deep into the ground.

I copied her action and jabbed mine into the soft earth too.

Djorki barked, he had gone some way in the direction the woodcutter had indicated and seemed to want us to follow. We followed tamely.

A couple of hundred paces further on we met a fast flowing stream almost a river. In the middle of the stream was a rocky outgrowth about six or seven yards in length. A huge oak grew on it.

From somewhere not far behind we heard the howl of a wolf. Ahwenda seemed to make a quick calculation as to the speed of the current, moved a little way upstream and a little back from the water's edge, took me under her right arm and ran leaping high, *Hold your breath*, she shouted.

Water came over my head it was icy cold. Memories sprang up in me of Monika, the Grey, Maria, of the first time I left the hamlet ... all my memories were waiting to gush forth.

Ahwenda held me tight and lifted my face above the water's surface. She was half swimming, half walking. The water reached up to her neck. We made the only place on the rock where we could climb out of the stream. I tried desperately to clamber up, she pushed me from behind then scrambled up herself.

As soon as she was out, she gestured for Djorki to go upstream.

I was shivering violently but saw a straight branch, or perhaps a long stave for it seemed to have been cut, leaning against the oak. I went to it and held onto it tightly to stop trembling.

She was motioning frantically to the dog. Djorki ran toward the stream and jumped. He was swimming toward our island but the current was strong and seemed to be carrying him past. She caught sight of the stake I was holding, yanked it out of my hands and thrust one end toward the dog. His teeth snapped onto it. Holding the other end she was able to draw him to the island and drag him out.

As Djorki began shaking water off him, I saw a pair of wolf eyes under the eaves of the trees. Three or four wolves appeared on the bank.

The sky above us was deep blue.

36. Surrounded

The wolves showed no urge to jump into the river and attack us. Ahwenda was desperately attempting to light a fire. Her gear was wet through, the tindering mechanism hardly able to make a spark. My grown-up self, which but a little while earlier had infused me, had departed. I was a seven year old, far from home, soaked, shivering and crying.

About ten wolves were gathered at the water's edge. Djorki stood facing them. Ahwenda had collected dry leaves and some dry twigs, her face was blurred as I looked at her through my tears.

The twin stone, she whispered drawing forth the stone Monika had given her. It was a slice of crystal, green around the edge becoming crimson in the centre. She clasped it tightly in her hands for a moment and closed her eyes almost as if she were praying. All at once she struck the twig with the crystal, a tiny flame flickered up. She repeated the action, flames sprang up more brightly. Once more and an even brighter flame appeared and kindled the twig. Quickly and expertly she worked to make a little fire. Luckily there was no wind. Watching the wolves intently Djorki growled in defiance.

The oak was partly hollow, I withdrew into it, sitting down to look at her tend the fire. As I leant back something stuck into me. I reached back and felt a branch. There was a bundle of branches stacked up and beside them deeper inside the hollow were chunks of dried wood, piled up as though placed there for fuel. I grabbed a piece of the wood and pointed to the stockpile as I spoke her name. Her face lit up with surprise and wonder as she saw the stock of wood. She leapt up broke a branch from the bundle and set both halves to the flames. Our little fire began to burn in earnest.

Djorki barked. We glanced across as a huge shaggy wolf appeared. The other wolves slunk away from it. This was the pack leader, bigger and broader with an aura of malice about it, unmistakably the descendent of a manipulated warg. It sniffed the air and howled. I drew behind Ahwenda and held onto her. Djorki barked back his challenge.

The warg began making throaty growls and bit one of the other wolves. The bitten wolf drew back then ran toward the stream and launched itself into the air. It cleared half the distance before landing in the water. It tried to swim toward us but the current carried it away.

The rock of our little island rose sheer four or five feet out of the water. Only at the place we had climbed out did it break apart. For the wolves to get at us they had to reach this point.

We stood watching them. I had grasped the long stave again and held it upright. The warg was snarling, it was possessed of cunning and able to communicate its commands to the rest of the pack. Another wolf sprang into the water from near to where Djorki had jumped. It looked as if it might make the climbing out point. Ahwenda took the stake from me and pushed the wolf away. The current carried it downstream.

She began working to build up the fire. The night was cold, the sky black. The moon had risen into sight when the warg howled again, rage and hunger for human flesh echoed in its cry. Again I clutched Ahwenda, again Djorki barked back his challenge. Then it sprang out into the river almost making the distance. Ahwenda thrust at its back with the stake. Even though swimming it was somehow able to twist and bite into the stave. With a jerk of its powerful neck it pulled, she cried out and had to let go of her end as she almost lost her balance. During the skirmish the current had carried the warg further downstream. The danger had passed but we had lost the stave.

The fire, she shouted, *We must build up the fire*.

The wood was dry and perfect for burning. The camp fire quickly blazed, the cold and dark were driven away.

So long as it burns so brightly they will not attack, she sat near the fire and drew me to her, *I will sing for you, Kell*.

As she began to sing softly, I felt myself tumbling into deep slumber. The last thing I noted was Djorki crouching not far from us, his eyes fixed on the wolves.

In spite of the night and being outside, and in spite of the danger, I slept as only a child could. A couple of times I was roused from slumber by Djorki's barking and saw Ahwenda with a blazing branch in either hand guarding the climbing-out point. Twice more wolves sought to swim to us and twice they were repelled by the fire sticks in her hands.

As morning drew near I lay with open eyes listening to the twitter of birds. This was not a sliced forest, the birds here were of the earth and not descended from manipulations. They joyously greeted the dawn with their chorus.

The camp fire still gave warmth. Ahwenda was boiling water in an enamelled cup. I glanced across to where the wolves had been and caught sight of a wolf under a tree.

They will watch and wait but wolves and especially wargs are creatures of the dark. They will not attack as long as the sun is shining and the fire burns.

I sat up at her words and glanced over at the wood pile.

It is half used but I think we shall be rescued today, little one.

Do they know we are here?

We have the stone, Monika has the twin. It is a kind of calling stone.

Can you call to each other with them?

I cannot. But she can discern through her stone what comes to pass around its twin. It was through her that I was able to bring forth flames. By itself the tourmaline has no power over fire. She took the cup. *The water is boiling, black tea and spices is what we need.*

I'm hungry.

We have a little supply of biscuits, we will not stave, she glanced at the dog which came over and started to lick her face. *Stop it, stop it*, she laughed.

In response to her laughter two wolves stepped up to the bank, behind them further in the shadow I caught sight of the warg. Djorki growled at them.

They hate our laughter, our joy, our freedom. But let us not think of them, the sun is shining and the tea hot.

We breakfasted upon tea with a nut biscuit and a few dried berries each.

Ahwenda took out her long hunting knife, climbed a little up the oak tree and cut a branch. Then she took from her rucksack a thin metal ring about two hand breadths across around which a net was threaded. With a thin cord she wound the ring to the branch. *A fishing net!* She held it up, *If I can catch a fish Djorki will not go hungry.*

She was standing at the climbing point, the net dipped in the water. Very still she stood. I went to hug the dog. After a few minutes she suddenly brought up the net and set a threshing fish on the rock. She knelt beside it knife in hand, the knife descended, the fish's movement ceased. Long she looked at it before shaking her head, *This will not do, it is descended from a manipulation*.

Almost angrily she grabbed the fish by its tail swung it

round her head and threw it high into the air toward the wolves. It landed near them, they began to fight over it. The warg shook itself and stepped forth. The two wolves drew back as it sniffed the fish. It made no attempt to eat.

It will not eat fish when human flesh is so near, she put her hand on my shoulder as she spoke.

The warg stood watching us. I was glad the fire was burning behind us. Its eyes seemed only half open as though it hated the light. As I looked deeper into its pupils dizziness came over me – fear – I felt I was falling toward it.

Ahwenda's hand gripped my shoulder more tightly as she spoke, *Wargs have more weapons than tooth and claw. Drink more tea.*

As the warg retreated into the shadow, trembling came over me. She sat down beside me and brought the still warm tea to my lips. I gazed into the dancing flames and felt ashamed that I had fallen under the hypnotic spell of its eye. My fingers took a grip of a stone, once more I sensed the closeness of my grown-up self. I imagined myself casting a stone and breaking the skull of the warg.

Ahwenda brought her face close to mine, peering at me intently, *You seem okay.*

I leapt up stone in hand and looked across to where the warg was crouched, *I will learn to fight such beasts.*

Good! And I will try to catch another fish for Djorki.

Five minutes later she pulled another fish out of the water. *A trout*, she said, *And not manipulated.* She cupped the dead fish in her hands and held it up. Djorki was near her, his mouth watering. She smiled at him, *Let us give thanks, we should not take life even for food without giving thanks.*

Then she placed the fish at his feet, the dog's saliva dripped on it but he made no attempt to eat until she gave him a sign.

Don't gobble it up too quickly and mind the bones. she turned to me, *On my next trip I shall remember to bring dog biscuits*.

The sun was westering. The wolves were returning to the bank and gazing over at us.

Ahwenda glanced anxiously at our dwindling stock of dry wood. *They may not rescue us today*, she said sadly as she drew forth the slice of crystal Monika had given her and whispered into it. She rose, the wind blew her hair over face *Kell, I know not what the night will bring but, but I believe you should know more*.

She sat down and drew me into her, and started to tell me more about Monika.

37. Lihana

Lihana, I will call her by the name she was once known as, was a genius in every respect. Russian, beautiful, intense, a natural singer whose voice could effortlessly fill a cathedral, a virtuoso of the violin, an expert pianist, a talented gymnast, she could draw, paint and sculpt exquisitely, she had mastered more than half a dozen non-Slavic languages – and all this while barely out of her teens. Her choice of study at university was mathematics. In her the spirit of Gauss, Abel and Galois seemed to have arisen in finer form. She avoided the sciences because, as she argued, their theories were built upon invalid hypotheses. She knew this because from an early age she had direct insight into the invisible worlds. She encountered the works of Stoner and began to read Mountain's books.

During her student days the world was in upheaval. The Falarch High Command – which for decades had orchestrated finance, pharmacy, technological innovation and production, guided national politics carefully into Falarch organised over-national frameworks and channelled culture into forms of electronic entertainment – finally began to expose itself. By this time she had moved to Switzerland pursuing post-doctoral studies. There she learnt to master Stoner's dance form as none known to the world had ever done before. She rediscovered Nick Thomas' books which had been ignored for decades and through his insights was able to explain how machines such as Keeley's, based on subtle reciprocal oscillations, were able to operate. She brought forth working models of machines, called Strader machines by Stoner's followers, such as the world had never seen. And she married and became the mother of five children.

She had met her husband in a spiritual centre near Basel, a man older than she was and a veritable knower of the Stoner archives. They had five children in quick succession. Life had been wonderful for her. Her husband borrowed money to build factories to produce her machines. But life changed abruptly when the Falarch High Command went openly for world dictatorship. Her husband preached the need to accommodate Falarch institutions, to bow to Falarch directives and censorship. And this even as Falarch mercenaries were butchering hundreds of thousands of people around the globe.

She could not accept his position. They became estranged. She was left to bring up her five children alone. He disappeared. It was rumoured that he accepted a post in the Falarch hierarchy.

Her two eldest children returned from stays abroad. Shortly after this open war broke out around the world as humankind united to throw off the Falarch yoke. She stepped into the Resistance and brought her machines into play. The Falarch armies floundered.

It was then– Ahwenda's head dropped, tears streamed from her eyes, *That they took her children.*

She had been called away. Her children were in a protected place. It should not have been possible for anyone to have broken in and taken them. Not unless the children themselves had let the intruders in. Some believed it was her former husband, the father to her children, who had come and convinced his own children to let him in.

Whatever had happened, when she returned she found her children gone and a ransom note, an electronic one, demanding that she turn over all her machines to the Falarch armies and henceforth to work for them – otherwise her children were to suffer terrible torture, experimentation and death.

To have given in to the demand was out of the question. Her machines and her expertise would have brought about millions of deaths and entrenched the Falarchs as the masters of humanity for a thousand-year reign. She quickly altered her machines so they could not be used. And turned herself over to the Falarch High Command. She refused to work for them until her children were returned to her. I do not know the drama, the threats, the bargaining – but somehow she managed to get her children brought to her. They were in an impregnable Falarch bunker guarded with battalions of elite troops armed with high-tech weapons, many of their top scientists worked there. Some near the very pinnacle off the Falarch hierarchy came to gloat. Yet none knew what Lihana was capable of, none knew the forces she could unleash. Who can tell the tale of how she broke the bunker and left it utterly destroyed. It is said that not one escaped its destruction except Lihana and her five children. They came from the ruins and returned to the Resistance.

Maybe she had broken esoteric laws in employing such forces but if so surely it was but a return to balancing, for they had first taken illicit action – they had attacked children. The Falarch leaders are as aware as we are of the rules governing engagement.

Overjoyed Lihana and her children were united with their friends ... and yet, and yet.

Ahwenda bowed her head, tears were streaming down her cheeks, *I*– her voice was hardly articulated, *I saw their end. I saw them die. The Grey showed me*. She sobbed uncontrollably.

It took some time for her composure to return so she could continue speaking, *They had operated capsules into her children. Three in each child containing chemical, viral and bacterial poisons which were released into their bodies shortly after the escape. Lihana did not realise what was happening until it was too late. She watched each of her children die in torment, one after another.*

As the last child died and even before the burial ceremonies, she left and returned to the compound from which her children had been taken hostage. She had already woven forces around this place making it more impregnable than a Falarch bunker. And then she began preparing to unleash forces such as had not been seen since the days of creation.

She could single handedly have destroyed the Falarch armies and the Falarch command posts. And yet, and yet, it would have been evilly done had she acted out her intentions. For she would have broken the rules of engagement and this would have allowed the remnants of the Falarch hierarchy to have brought forth powers of destruction pent up in the core of the earth. In the ensuing wars maybe even the earth herself would have been destroyed.

None in the Resistance could have stopped her. And perhaps the Masters of the Falarchs were willing her to take the step.

Then he came. No one knew where he came from nor how he was able to neutralise the compound's defences. A boy only twelve years old, he knocked upon her door – and she stood before him.

Had he not been a child she might have struck him down there and then. But she could not bring herself to kill a boy. I am too exhausted to relate their speech, Kell. Suffice it to say that she recognised him, she recognised that he was a true representative of the Highest even though still a child who had not reached his teens.

She poured out her pain, her anger, her lust for revenge, her anguish, her tears. He held her for hours in his arms.

Who was he? I asked.

Do you really not know?

We spoke his name in unison, *The Grey.*

Michaelleon, he called himself then, the Lion of Michael.

He had come to her in the darkest hour of the night. At dawn another Visitor came. One that no defences can hinder. He stood with the glow of his majesty behind them. The Grey wanted to touch the Visitor's feet but was stopped. The Man put his arms around their shoulders and whispered to them. Just before he departed with a shimmer of glory followed by his complete disappearance, he asked them, "Be friends for my sake, and work for the good only by the means of goodness".

The boy, Michaelleon, nodded his ascent and Lihana whispered, "Yes".

As the Visitor left, she fell into a deep sleep.

I know this to be true, Kell, because the Grey took me to witness the event within the memory of the world. Yet to this day I do not know if she consciously remembers what occurred. And I have never dared to ask her.

We fell silent. The sun had descended below the height of the trees. Night would soon be upon us.

There is one more thing I must tell you. Michaelleon brought her a message, he told Lihana something neither she nor anyone else knew. Her eldest children, a boy and a girl were twins. During the year before open war broke out and they were taken hostage, both of them had been away. The girl for a year, the boy for half a year. The girl in Russia. The boy here in Scandinavia. The boy fathered a child. He did not know he was to be a father. His child was born after he was dead. The girl bore a babe and left it in Russia. She had meant to tell her mother, she had meant to return to the babe. But events were moving with great speed, she never found the right moment to speak. A couple of months after she returned from Russia, all of Lihana's children were taken hostage.

Ahwenda looked at me in great earnest, *I am sprung from the babe of Lihana's daughter. You and Maria from the child of Lihana's son.*

You mean we are Monika's, er Lihana's grandchildren?

Ahwenda burst out laughing, long and free she laughed, *How strange that one can laugh so fully when–* she gestured toward the wolves. *No, Kell, not her grandchildren. We are her great grandchildren.*

Are there others?

Not that I know of. But they would never tell me even if there were.

She stood up and gazed at the heavens, the Western sky was red, *We must prepare, the night is near.*

38. The Second Night

Ahwenda began hacking branches from the oak tree with her long hunting knife. *I cannot cut through thick branches, this is a knife not an axe, and it needs to be kept sharp. I have left it late, I fear.* The woods were still, only the sounds came from her knife. She threw down a branch muttering bitterly, *I thought they would have come for us today.*

One or two stars were twinkling. The wind was beginning to blow causing the fire to blaze up. Only about a quarter of the dry wood was left.

Pick up the branches, Kell, and lay them near the fire so they can start to dry. She was up in the oak still slashing at the tree.

The wolves were lined up on the bank. As the blue faded into black, the warg stirred itself and came to the water's edge. Djorki stood directly opposite. I moved to his side and gazed at the warg. As I looked into its eyes, I sensed a change in me. Once again it was as though my grown-up self drew closer. I was able to peer into its cavernous pupils without being possessed by fear or in danger of being hypnotised.

The warg sat on its haunches and snarled. One by one the wolves began to howl. As one finished another would begin. Djorki started to bark at them furiously.

Ahwenda leapt down from the tree and patted him, *Let them howl, stay by us*, she said to our dog.

As the moon rose over the trees the great warg himself howled. All the wolves joined in chorus. Djorki's deep bark answered them. As the chorus of howling died, Ahwenda began to sing. Her voice rose, I recognised the language, it was a stirring Russian song, one Monika often sang. Then I noticed a second change in me. Not only was

I near myself, something higher than my adult self, something even more truly me which would always hover above me and never fully come into me, yet something which in the far future I knew I could become, this higher self drew close to me.

We stood side by side, maid, boy and dog. We would not be cowered by the howls of wolves. The warg snarled again and moved off, the wolves followed him upstream. One of the wolves jumped into the river.

Djorki stay, do not attack! Kell tend the fire, get a branch to burn.

Ahwenda stood at the climbing-out point, knife in hand. As the wolf clawed at the rock she slashed across it muzzle. It cried out in pain and was carried past by the current. A second wolf had already dived into the water. It too received the knife. By the time the fifth wolf swam toward us Ahwenda had a blazing branch in her hand, she had only to push the flame toward its face to stop it swimming on.

It all seemed too easy. Even Djorki no longer stood, he crouched down watching the defeated wolves being carried away by the stream.

The wolves returned from the water only to receive the biting punishment of the warg. Sometimes it would bite the ears of the wolves. Sometimes it set its great jaws around their throats as though threatening them with death.

The second time they attacked was far worse. When she thrust a flaming branch into their faces they swam on, fur and flesh burning but more afraid of the warg than of the fire. Only the sudden sweep of Ahwenda's knife across their muzzles finally stopped their course.

I began to feel sorry for the wolves caught between the warg and Ahwenda, between its teeth and her knife. They were not modified creatures, they were wolves unfortunate enough to have a warg as a pack leader, a leader which lusted not for sheep or deer but for the blood of humankind.

On their second return from the water, the warg held each of them long by the throat. One of the wolves snarled in defiance and backed away. The warg held its gaze until its resistance drained away and then it struck, its teeth ripped out the other wolf's throat.

Maybe they will kill each other?

No chance of that, and even if they do, the warg itself is more dangerous than all the other wolves together.

As she spoke, I saw how drawn and tired she looked. And I knew it was not just fatigue that drained her but the necessity of inflicting wounds.

We had no more fire branches. Our fuel was low, hardly enough for more than an hour. The moon had risen to its zenith when the warg howled. Long it howled and as its cry died away, it ran toward us and sprang into the water. Ahwenda stood with her knife at the climbing point. Djorki barked.

My adult self had never left me this night and my higher self had never been far from my heart, yet as the warg had launched itself across the water, a third change took place in me. A presence of purest selflessness drew into me, a non-trespassing being nearer to myself than my very self, a being for whom time is both simultaneity and duration, one for whom a second is as slow moving as an hour, a year no longer than a day. I now knew the source of the slowing down of time.

The warg was at the climbing point, Ahwenda had not struck, perhaps she remembered how it had taken the stave between in its teeth, perhaps she was waiting for the right instant.

Strike Ahwenda, I shouted.

The warg somehow brought itself up out of the water and snapped at her leg, she threw herself backwards and rolled over. The warg would have taken her had not Djorki attacked. Yet in spite of being hardly out of the water and lower down, its speed and strength allowed it to push Djorki back.

The warg reached the level rock. It was far longer and stronger than our dog. Djorki was bleeding but barking back at it. Ahwenda had risen to her feet, knife in hand. The warg was motionless, for an instant its eye flickered toward me and I sensed its intention: to rip out the still beating child heart from my breast.

But for me all this was taking place with extreme slowness. I knew what I had to do. I had already drawn the calling stone from my pocket and I threw it in a motion which for me in this state of grace was smooth and strong but which for the world around me must have taken place with a rapidity to make the movement of a Rikki Tikki Tavi seem like that of a sloth's. The stone left my hand with a whirr but part of me never separated from its line of motion. As the warg drew back to launch its attack, the stone buried itself deep in its eye.

The selfless non-trespassing presence began to withdraw but still the movements around me seemed slow. The warg cried out in pain, Djorki attacked and took it by the throat, Ahwenda with a bound and downward thrust plunged her blade into its chest, its blood spurted out all over her.

The warg shrieked in it death throes – and it was ended.

I called out to the other wolves, *Keep away from wargs in future*.

My adult and my higher self were likewise returning to their place of sanctuary. I became once more a seven year old. But I knew one more thing needed doing, Ahwenda and Djorki had to wash away the poisonous spittle and blood of the warg. I picked up the enamelled cup and filled it from the stream.

She was on her knees, *How could I not have struck when I had the chance, I endangered us all.*

Wash Ahwenda, get the blood of the warg off you, my voice sounded commanding, almost reminiscent of Monika herself, *I will wash Djorki.*

She obeyed my order. Our dog was still bleeding from his muzzle which had taken the teeth of the warg.

With her last strength Ahwenda instructed me how to tend the camp fire so it would burn through the night in spite of the shortage of fuel. She lay down near the fire, Djorki came to her, his whimpers reminded me of Mutty's when it had been bitten by a spliced rat.

39. The Rescue Party

The night was old, the fire low, I was its sole guardian. She had fallen into a fitful sleep. There was no wind. The stars directly overhead shone clear and cold. I was standing gazing up at the heavens as I spoke aloud, *Please, Djorki and Ahwenda have been so good and brave, please don't let them die*, I knew I was begging the presence of purest selflessness.

No change in my experience of time came about but deep inside I felt what had to be done. I stumbled to the climbing point and nearly fell in. It would have been my end for I had not learnt to swim. I was trembling as I knelt to take water into the enamelled cup. Back at the fireside I mixed earth with water and moulded mud in my hand. Then I smeared mud on Ahwenda's face and a little on Djorki's nose. He opened his eyes, pain shone out of them. I threw the last wood onto the fire and snuggled up to Ahwenda.

Just before I fell asleep, I pictured the Angel of the Dogs descending and lifting Djorki to the heavens in supplication.

The sound of voices wakened me. The sun had risen. Three men dressed like Rangemen were standing on the bank. They called out to me. I rose up and stared at them, and returned no greeting.

We seek Ahwenda, one of them shouted.

Who are you, I shouted back.

We are Rangemen of course.

I felt sick and wondered why they hadn't come for us yesterday if they were Rangemen. My voice was surly, *How do I know that you are not Falarch servants?*

They broke out in merry laughter. An older man

dressed differently in green and deep blue, came out of the trees. They addressed him, *Herr Lindremann, the lad here thinks we might be Falarchs!*

He peered over to us, *Ahwenda is with you and an injured dog.*

Neither she nor Djorki had stirred. I glanced down at them, tears streaming down my cheeks.

One of the Rangemen called out, *How did you reach the island?*

We swam.

The youngest of the men striped off most of his clothing and dived in. He never reached the climbing-out point, the current took him downstream. His comrades were in fits of laughter as he was forced to swim in to the bank further downstream. Their merriment more than anything stilled my doubts about who they were.

You must be powerful swimmers, the young Rangeman shouted.

We jumped in further upstream, even the wolves had the sense to do that.

Again his comrades started laughing.

Only on his third attempt did he reach the landing point and climb out. Meanwhile Lindremann was instructing the others to cut and bind branches. They were to make a kind of bridge.

In spite of not being young Lindremann was the second to walk over the makeshift bridge. He glanced at the warg and then knelt beside Ahwenda. After half a minute he turned to me with a sharp question, *Have you cast them into a magic sleep, lad?*

Ain't done nothin'

They sleep so unnaturally naturally.

A brawny Rangeman, who I sensed was a leader, crossed over to us, he too knelt beside Ahwenda, *Are they ill?* There was concern in his deep voice.

I don't rightly know. They are sleeping peacefully. But they have taken the blood and spittle of a spliced wolf, he glanced at the carcass, *A great warg at that. If only the Grey were here or Lihana.*

Lihana wouldn't be able to save them.

Lindremann jumped to his feet, *You, lad, have no notion of what Lihana can do!*

She couldn't save Dungbjorn's dog when it was bitten by a spliced rat.

He stared at me.

Prayers saved the dog not medicines.

And have your prayers put them into this sleep, boy?

They need black tea with spices and a spoonful of honey if you have it.

The big Rangeman broke in a grin, *Well Lindrmann, is the lad teaching the healer how to heal?*

Ahwenda stirred, *Tea*, she whispered, *Black tea with spices and syrup.*

She began scratching her arm. Lindremann drew up her sleeve, her left forearm was red and swollen. The fangs of the warg must have punctured her skin. He felt her forehead.

She opened her eyes and focused on him, *Lindremann, I, but, but where is Kell?*

Djorki had opened his eyes too. I recognised the look in them, it was the same as Mutty's on the morning after he had been tended. They were safe. I broke into sobs and threw myself down between them.

The big Rangeman bore Ahwenda over the bridge. Djorki was more trouble, they had to make a briar to bear him over. Lindremann kept me on the island for questioning.

Well now lad, I want to hear more about what

happened. This is a great warg and deadlier than that they do not come, unless– his voice faded, he shook his head. His piercing blue eyes bore into me, *How was it slain?*

Ahwenda and Djorki slew it.

Did they now?

Djorki took it by the throat and Ahwenda stabbed it through the heart.

Did they now? He was inspecting the warg's body, *And what have we here?*

It's mine. I went to take it.

He grabbed my arm, *Careful now, let me.* He took pincers and pulled out the stone, rubbed it on the earth and washed it clean with fresh water. *Water and earth are good against splicings*. He examined the black stone, *But this is a calling stone!*

It's not finished. Raynor gave it to me. Monika, er Lihana, said I could keep it.

Keep it then, he handed it back to me.

Now tell me again how the warg was slain.

I repeated my story.

But how did the stone strike the eye of the warg?

I stared back at him in silence, in resolute silence.

Well, well, we might never get to the bottom of this, his eyes twinkled, *But I am old enough to know that there are some things I will never fully comprehend.*

The big Rangeman called Blarney (his grandmother had been Irish) returned to us, *Shall I carry the lad across.*

I'll walk over. I said it with sullen certainty.

It was a bad decision, I was a seven year old trying to be a teenager. Halfway across the swaying construction I lost balance and fell, Blarney tried to grab me but couldn't hold on. I was underwater and surging downstream, and very afraid. My head broke the surface. I heard Djorki's bark and Ahwenda shout, *Kell, he can't swim.*

The young Rangeman was running down the bank parallel to me, he dived in to save me, fully clothed this time.

They were all laughing when we came dripping up to the fire.

I had taken off my wet clothes and sat shivering under a blanket. Lindremann came up with black tea with spices and a spot of tree-syrup sugar. I took the drink and burnt my tongue. Ahwenda sipped her tea quietly.

Lindremann put his arm on my shoulder, *And now lad, tea for people but what about the dog, what does your healer's sense tell you he needs?*

A dog biscuit.

Lindremann had seen to the burning of the great warg. The fire on the island was still smouldering but the camp fire of the Rangemen had been covered with soil. We began to move off. I walked beside Ahwenda, both she and Djorki were being borne on stretchers.

Kell, I will tell everyone how your throw saved us.

No, no, Ahwenda, please you must promise me not to, you must promise, I held so tightly onto the hand of her injured arm that she cried out in pain.

But why?

I can't tell you now – but promise me, promise me, promise me!

Okay, my little saviour angel, I promise.

I sighed with relief. It would have been a crime to have taken credit for the presence of purest selflessness. But I couldn't speak of this to Ahwenda, not even to Monika.

We had gone about two or three hundred paces through the trees when I realised something, *Stop*, I shouted, *Stop we are going the wrong way!*

Everyone stopped. Blarney, who had been leading,

strode back to us and gave me a stern glance, *Well boy, is a little seven year old who can't swim and can't walk over a bridge without falling, telling Rangemen which trail to take?*

I bowed my head, *It's just that there's something I have to check.*

Lindremann was by my side, he spoke up for me, *If there's something this lad wants observe, I want to see it too.*

Blarney shrugged his shoulders. And we began to move off in another direction.

What is it, Kell, where do you want to go? Ahwenda whispered.

To where we met the old woodcutter.

Oh!

I was looking around desperately trying to remember where we had seen him. Then I caught sight of our two branches.

Delicate white blossom covered the branches we had thrust into the earth.

But it is Autumn, Blarney mumbled as he stared at the blossom in disbelief.

Lindremann dug his elbow into the big Rangeman, *More things in heaven and earth, eh Blarney*, he winked at me.

I whispered to Ahwenda, *Shall we take them with us?*

She was silent for a moment then shook her head, *Let them take root here, let these blossoming branches bless this little wood.*

40. A Second Hamlet

I was lying beside Ahwenda on her stretcher as we neared a low hill. All at once I detected something dark and ominous, and sat up. The Rangemen bearing us stepped under arching Rowan trees and the atmosphere altered, I realised we must have entered the sanctuary of a second hamlet.

This was built on, or perhaps better said into the hillock. The dwellings were what I later came to think of as hobbit-like. And a warren of passageways and storage rooms had been excavated behind the people's homes near the surface. To the North behind the crown of the hill, were surface buildings: Homesteads, barns and even a little hospital run by the healers. This second hamlet was far bigger and more complicated than the one I had grown up in.

We were taken to an isolation cottage close to the hospital. The three of us, Ahwenda, me and Djorki shared a room. Lindremann lit a fire in our quarters before retiring to his own study on the other side of the cottage.

We had arrived in the afternoon and were given leave to sleep until evening. I woke first and gazed out of the window, the weather was cloudy, the fire had burnt low, the room was a little chilly. Ahwenda murmured to me, I went and lay beside her in her bed.

Tell me what happened after?

After what?

After the Grey and Monika, I mean Lihana, became friends.

She lay staring at the ceiling her blue-green eyes touched by sorrow, *Then the wars became open. Numerous people hardly known to the world but who harboured special talents and deeper connections to the angels or to elemental beings came to join the Resistance. Lihana built machines which were capable of breaking the deepest bunkers of the Falarchs. The bunkers would shake, the shaking would increase until they collapsed. They say that Tesla had once made a similar machine in the early twentieth century.*

Men and women over the whole earth felt a resurge of hope. Then– her voice trailed off, *Then they began releasing modified organisms in great quantities: Bacteria, vira, fungal cells – plants and animals died in huge numbers. And people, people began dying everywhere, in millions, tens, hundreds of millions. We had no defences against these modified strains. Then came the wargs, modified insects, trans-creatures bearing for instance bird, bat and beetle characteristics. Their scientists got hold of dinosaur DNA and redesigned dinosaurs.*

Though billions of people died, the Falarch High Command was broken and their armies began dispersing. But the manipulations, they had released, began to thrive and prey on nature's own species. And high-standing Falarchs seemed to possess power to control the modified beasts.

Once more she fell silent.

And then?

And then, oh Kell, they had long been experimenting with people. They brought forth Untermenschen, deformed human beings, people who didn't appear to have true individuality. They were able to work and understand, they had a fairly rudimentary speech and were governed by Falarch captains. They could be formed into suicidal battalions and were capable of killing and maiming without seeming to be touched by conscience. We call them the Hordes.

Ahwenda shook her head sadly before she continued, *Lihana's oscillation machines destroyed the Falarch arms production and could make aeroplanes or drones explode in mid air. The weaponry of the twentieth and twenty-first century was mostly destroyed as were the centres of industrial production. Civilisation no longer functioned. More than ninety percent of the world's population died in the space of twenty or thirty years. Great tracts of land became waste and there spliced creatures roam unopposed.*

As what remained of the Falarch forces sought to rebuild their bunkers and laboratories, the Resistance brought about the Oases. Only in the Oases are there oscillation machines and here culture is redeveloping. Here there are academies where mathematics, music, arts and true science blossom. The remnants of the Falarch armies have their own centres where they breed and train the Hordes.

Ahwenda put her head in her hands, I took one of her hands, she turned to me with a wry smile and spoke on, *It is no longer easy for human beings to bear children. In the Blighted Lands – between the Oases and the Falarch controlled Horde breeding colonies – live men, women and children who belong neither to us nor to the Falarchs. Their numbers are ever dwindling. They are ravaged by manipulated creatures and by marauding Hordes. They can no longer grow food, they have returned to hunter-gatherer existences. Though we seek to build hamlets, villages which are fortified and protected by Rangemen in these lonely lands. At times the Hordes march against the hamlets and sometimes even against the Oases.*

But how are the wars going, Ahwenda? Will we win or will the Falarchs?

Do you remember what the Visitor said to the boy

Michaelleon and Lihana?

Yes, he said, er–

She finished the sentence for me, *Work for the good by means of goodness. What characterises the Falarch controlled forces is that they seek to achieve their aims by all possible means.* She repeated this last phrase with emphasis, *By all possible means. We on the other hand cherish human freedom. We will never force anyone to choose us or to choose the good.*

Ahwenda, does it make it easier for them because they will do anything to win?

She frowned and took me in her arms, *Not easier, I think, because if given a truly free choice human beings always tend to choose the good. The Falarchs just make it harder to choose the good. You can no longer choose the good and expect to live an easy life lazing about and enjoying creature comforts. The Grey once told me to read 'Lord of the Rings' nine times – once for each of the members of the Fellowship, I suppose. He said inside knowledge of this book gives great protection against falling prey to Falarch schemes. To choose the good – or to choose the easy way out, that was how the Grey put it. But he also added, 'Remember you do not fight alone'.*

There was a knock on the door, Lindremann peered in, *Are you hungry – or perhaps I should ask, What does our little healer recommend?* His blue eyes were twinkling.

Thoughts of Monika's tree-syrup sweets came into my mind, Duncan, Victor – but then I remembered that I had resolved not to eat them. I put on a grown-up voice, *A little vegetable soup and, em, unleavened bread and freshly drawn spring water.*

Lindremann bowed, *Your recommendations are in line with my own! Would you like to eat in bed?*

He entered the room and without waiting for a reply,

put a bowl of water in front of Djorki and took a dog biscuit out of his pocket. We ate in our room. Djorki looked a lot healthier and Ahwenda less tired.

We were lying in our beds, a candle was lit, Ahwenda was singing to me in Russian. She reached out her hand to me, I squeezed it and slipped out from my bed and in under her sheets.

Ahwenda, I've been thinking about what would have happened if Lihana had taken the Grey for a Falarch intruder and struck him down?

You are a lot quicker than me, Kell, it took me half a year before I formulated that particular question and asked him. And then a further fortnight went by before he answered me. He said, he might risk his own life but not the earth's, and that he had made the link with her even before she came to door. I didn't know what he meant, he had to explain: If she had attacked him he would not have lifted a finger to defend himself but if he had died, she would have been irresistibly drawn across the threshold of death with him.

I shuddered, *But what if they were not here, how would we able to defend ourselves against–?*

We should have to put all our faith in the Visitor, I suppose.

We were silent for a while, my head was leaning against her arm.

Ahwenda?

Not more questions!

Just one, why aren't there more of us, why has Monika, er Lihana only three great grandchildren?

I don't know, Kell. It's harder for people to have children than it once was just a few years ago and, and– she glanced earnestly down at me.

Tell me, tell me!

Yes, perhaps you have a right to know. Falarch forces are hunting us.

Because Monika is out grandmother? Do they think we might have inherited her powers? Do they want to destroy us?

Yes, well, no– She sat up in bed, drew me to her and pulled the bedclothes tightly around us, *It's more complicated, I don't know for certain but I think that they think we might go either way.*

Either way?

Remain with the good or– she kissed my forehead.

Or?

Or seek to win by all possible means. Remember we spring not only from Lihana but also from her husband. And even she herself went too far. They wish to capture us and make us work for them – they want to make us part of the Falarch hierarchy.

I shuddered.

She hugged me tightly, *I have said too much you are only seven. You must sleep.* She reached across and blew out the candle.

My heart went out to my sister. Were they seeking for her too? I imagined dark fingers grasping across the sea for her. Ahwenda began to hum a Celtic lullaby.

I awoke in my own bed, Djorki noticed me moving and came to lick my face. Ahwenda was still peacefully sleeping. The door opened cautiously, Lindremann looked in. He came and knelt beside my bed as he spoke, *Today you should get up.*

We heard an outer door open and close. A moment later the big Rangeman entered, *Lindremann, an army of the Hordes is marching North. The Grey is seeking to hinder their approach. I have received unconfirmed reports that the hamlet to the South of the spliced forest is razed but that Lihana is leading the villagers North.*

I pictured the men and women of the hamlet marching with Monika. And Dungbjorn with his dog beside him carrying Miss and Moppar in a cat basket.

Lindremann looked up at the serious face of the Rangeman and nodded.

Blarney lowered his voice, *It is rumoured that the Sophianic seeresses are forming the Great Circle, Light is pouring into the Oasis of Trondheim.*

Sophianic seeresses, I whispered, and the eyes, face and falling hair of my little sister, Maria, were vividly before me.

Here ends Book One of the series 'the Oases and the Hordes'. Book Two is entitled 'The Light of Trondheim'.